At the bottom of the mall, I turned to head across the dock toward the speedboat, but I lost my footing and fell down, my face smashing into the concrete. Pat immediately scrambled away from me.

I jumped up as one of Seidelman's men raced across the dock directly at me. I had just enough time to sidestep his charge and drive my fist into his solar plexus.

He doubled over, and as he started to go down, I hammered both fists into the back of his neck.

Six of Seidelman's goons were on me then, their fists smashing at my face, neck and chest.

Before I went down I managed to kick one of them in the groin, but then a fist the size of a side of beef seemed to materialize out of nowhere. It hammered me in the face and everything went dark. I heard Pat scream somewhere off to my right. . . .

NICK CARTER IS IT!

"Nick Carter out-Bonds James Bond."
—*Buffalo Evening News*

"Nick Carter is America's #1 espionage agent."
—*Variety*

"Nick Carter is razor-sharp suspense."
—*King Features*

"Nick Carter is extraordinarily big."
—*Bestsellers*

"Nick Carter has attracted an army of addicted readers . . . the books are fast, have plenty of action and just the right degree of sex . . . Nick Carter is the American James Bond, suave, sophisticated, a killer with both the ladies and the enemy."
—*The New York Times*

FROM THE NICK CARTER
KILLMASTER SERIES

RETREAT FOR DEATH

An Ace Charter Original.

"Nick Carter" is a registered trademark of The Condé Nast Publications, Inc., registered in the United States Patent Office.

First Ace Charter Printing August 1982
Published simultaneously in Canada
Manufactured in the United States of America
2 4 6 8 0 9 9 7 5 3 1

RETREAT FOR DEATH

ONE

At ten thousand feet the Maryland countryside looked like a relief map, with toy houses and toy cars, a smudge on the horizon to the south, the toy city of Washington, D.C.

The wind tore at the open door as I stood on the edge, looking down.

Overhead, on the bulkhead, the light turned from red to amber, and I made sure my timer was set to zero and my altimeter agreed with the overhead dial.

The light winked green, and I stepped out, pushing myself slightly forward, and I was falling.

For just a moment I went unstable, heading for a tumbling fall, but then I was gliding, spread eagle, with little or no feeling of speed, only the wind buffeting my body.

It was mid-winter and very cold so that my face began to go numb, and my fingers in the thin gloves were stiffening up. But I loved it, and when Hap Thurmond, our Washington-based training coordinator had asked if I wanted to participate in the exercise, I had immediately agreed.

I was between assignments at the moment, and

in fact, David Hawk, the director of AXE, had told me three days ago to take a vacation.

Working as the nightside duty station chief, when little or nothing was going on, was boring, and I had decided to head south somewhere for a couple of weeks as soon as this exercise was completed.

For two days now, flying out of the CIA's field in Langley, we had run exercises, jumping from as low as one thousand feet, to as high as twenty thousand on oxygen.

Today's jump, according to Thurmond, was going to be a bit of a surprise.

I was just about to glance down at my timer, when something slammed into my back, knocking the wind out of me, and flipping me totally out of balance, so that for a wild second or two I was tumbling completely out of control.

I caught a glimpse of at least three figures above and beside me, before I had flipped back into a stable position, and then someone from far above hit me like an eagle swooping down on its prey, and the two of us were out of control.

Whoever it was on top of me, had one arm around my throat and his legs wrapped around my waist.

I tried to twist around to break his grip, but then there was a cold rush of air on my back, and he released me and pushed away, with my main and emergency parachute packs.

The straps around my legs and shoulders came loose in my hands from where he had cut them, and when I looked up and around, I could see that I was surrounded by four men in dark flight suits, all of them in freefall with me, but all of them equipped with chutes.

One of them broke away from the others, tightened up his body position and began to accelerate down and to the east, away from me. In his right hand he carried a spare chute.

The panorama of the Maryland countryside, which seconds before had seemed so lovely and inviting, now seemed terribly close and threatening.

I tightened up my body position and glided down toward the rapidly retreating figure of the diver with the spare chute as the other four grinned and waved wildly at me.

Thurmond, it was rumored around AXE headquarters, was totally insane. At one time, he had held a killmaster designation just like mine, for the super secret action-intelligence agency. Although Hawk would never talk about it, confirming or denying any of the rumors, most of us believed that Thurmond had gone around the bend on an assignment in China, nearly bringing the entire world into a nuclear confrontation.

He had supposedly been pulled off operational status, but because he knew too much, he had not been put out to pasture; instead he had been given the job of keeping operational field men, such as myself, in top physical and mental shape.

But this now, was too much, even by Thurmond's standards.

My altimeter and timer pack had been stripped away with my parachutes, but I didn't need them to know that I was coming dangerously close to an altitude where even with a parachute it would be too late.

The diver was expecting me, and as I began matching speeds with him, he looked up, grinned, and released my parachute pack. He peeled off to the west, popped his own chute, and was gone above me.

I concentrated, then, only on reaching the falling parachute pack. Moments later I reached it and quickly pulled it on, tightened the straps, and yanked the ripcord.

But nothing happened. I looked up in time to see the other three divers coming down fast toward me as I clawed open the pilot chute's cover, grabbed a handful of the silk and fed it out.

For a maddening second nothing happened, but then the wind caught the chute, it spun up and out, dragging the main chute with it, and I was jerked violently upright, the ground only a few hundred feet below me.

Just before I hit, I looked up. One chute was a few hundred yards to the east, and the other three were almost directly above me.

I hit hard, rolling with it, and instantly I leaped up and popped the quick release on my harness. I raced across the farm field toward where the other diver was going to land.

It usually takes a very long time for me to lose my temper, but the quickest way to cause me to is for someone to do something very stupid and very dangerous.

The other diver, coming down now for his landing, had qualified in spades on both accounts.

He landed near the edge of the farm field while I was still about fifty yards away, and by the time I reached him, he had popped his own quick release and was standing there calmly waiting for me.

It was Thurmond himself. I hadn't realized he was in the aircraft.

"What the hell was that all about?" I shouted.

He was laughing. "That was a good job, Nick. You did just fine."

"I did just fine?" I couldn't believe what I was hearing. "Why, for Christ's sake?"

"I thought you might have been going a little soft. You haven't been out on an operation in nearly four months."

I stepped a little closer to him. "Training for a specific operation is one thing," I said. "We're geared for it. But this now, today, was sheer insanity."

"What? Nick Carter *is* going soft on me—" Thurmond started to say, when I bunched up my right fist and hit him in the mouth with everything I had.

His head snapped back, and he went down, but just for a moment, before he jumped back up with a razor-sharp parachute rigger's knife in his right hand.

I backed up a step. Thurmond was about ten years older than me, but the man was as hard as nails, and a world-ranking expert in several martial arts, including the use of a knife. Besides, he technically was on our side.

"Hap!" shouted one of the other divers, as he approached us running across the field. The others were right behind him.

"Stay back!" Thurmond screamed.

"For God's sake, man!" one of the other training officers shouted.

"I'll kill you all!" Thurmond screamed, spittle flying from his mouth.

I held out my right hand. "All right, Hap, the game is over now," I said. "Put down the knife."

He lunged at me, and I had to quickly sidestep to avoid the slash of his knife. I knew what was coming then. I had been in enough hand-to-hand combat with the man; so I feinted to the left, as I had been taught to do, but instead of following through with the classic maneuver as I had been taught, and pulling back to the right, I continued to the left, falling to the ground and tumbling away, as Thurmond swung the blade right.

He realized his mistake, and started to pivot toward me, when one of his officers came up behind him and clipped him neatly behind the right ear with the butt of his pistol.

Thurmond went down like a felled ox, and he lay there unconscious.

"Jesus Christ," one of the officers swore, "what the hell happened?"

"I hit him," I said.

"No, I mean up there with the parachute?"

I turned to him. "You tell me what happened, Don," I snapped.

"It wasn't part of the training scenario. I swear it, Nick."

One of the other officers was shaking his head. "I didn't know what the hell the crazy bastard was up to," he said. "He was supposed to hit you, grab your chute, back off until you stabilized, and then hand you the spare he was carrying."

"We didn't know what the hell to think when he took off like that," Don said.

I glanced down at Thurmond who was still unconscious. "How far from the target zone are we?"

Don looked around to get his bearings. "Just past the line of trees over there to the west." He said. "A mile, maybe."

"All right, give me a hand with him then," I said. "This training exercise is over with."

"Yes, sir," Don said wholeheartedly.

It was late, well after six P.M., by the time we got Thurmond back to the dispensary at Langley, where the doctor said he probably had a mild concussion and would be out through the night at least. And it was well after eight by the time I had changed my clothes, retrieved my car and drove back into Washington, to AXE headquarters on DuPont Circle.

I parked in the sub-basement garage of the Amalgamated Press and Wire Services Building. AXE's worldwide operational front, and took the elevator up to the duty room on the third floor.

AXE, as a separate entity from the Central Intelligence Agency, and from all the other similar services within the U.S. government and military establishment, has been in existance since the fifties. It came about during the McCarthy witch hunts, when the CIA suddenly found itself hamstrung for lack of autonomy. There were too many watchdogs on what the service was doing. Things got much worse as time went on, and in the sixties and seventies when the CIA came under even harsher fire, AXE thrived.

Answerable only to the President and his council of security advisers, AXE has no charter as such, like the CIA. Instead, our job is to be always ready, willing and able to handle anything that needs to be done, at any time and in any place.

There is, as far as we're aware, no other government in the world that fields such a service.

The nightside crew was well into its shift as I stepped off the elevator and crossed the large room to my office in a glass-enclosed cubicle.

Rudolph Schmidt, the foreign desk analyst, looked up as I passed.

"Your phone's been ringing off the hook all afternoon," he said.

I went back to his desk and took the pile of telephone message slips from him. They were all from the same person, Pat Staley. I hadn't seen her in a couple of years. At one time we had been pretty close, when she had worked for us as a low-level cryptographer. She had quit the agency when her parents were killed in an airplane accident and had gone to work for the Staley Foundation, managing her parents' huge estate.

"She sounded a little anxious," Schmidt said, sitting back. He was grinning.

"Did she say she was in town?" I asked. She lived now in New York City.

"There's a number there. I think it might be the Marriott."

"Okay, thanks, Schmidty," I said. "Is Hawk still here?"

"No, he left an hour ago, but he told me to tell you if you came in that he would take care of Thurmond, whatever that means."

"Thanks," I said. "Anything happening around here tonight?"

"Nothing much," he said.

I nodded and went the rest of the way across the room and into my office where I sat down behind my desk, lit myself a cigarette, and then dialed the number Pat had left for me.

It was answered on the second ring. "Good evening, Twin Bridges Mariott."

"I'd like to speak with a Miss Pat Staley," I said. "I believe she's registered there."

"One moment please," the operator said.

Pat had to be about thirty now, and I had always thought she was one of the more beautiful women I had ever known. She was bright and fiercely independent, and yet she had never been one of those strident women liberationists. She knew who she was, what her abilities were, and she had never felt the need to go out and prove anything to anyone.

"Hello," her voice came on the line moments later.

"Pat?" I said. "This is Nick Carter."

"Thank God you've called, Nick," she said in a rush. She definitely sounded worried.

"What's the matter, Pat?" I asked.

"I really need your help, Nick," she said. "Can you come over right away?"

"I can be there in fifteen minutes. How about dinner right there?"

"Fine, fine, I don't care, just get here, Nick," she said, obviously very upset.

"Can you tell me now what's wrong?" I asked.

"No," she said tersely. "Just get over here. I'll meet you at the bar."

"I'll be there," I said, and she hung up.

I slowly put the phone back on the cradle and sat

back in my chair for a moment. Something was wrong. She had sounded nearly hysterical, as if she was on the verge of a breakdown.

She had taken her parents' deaths pretty hard, and for a time she had seen a psychiatrist. But there had been nothing wrong with her. Just normal grief.

Up in New York City, from what I had heard, she had done well with her parents' foundation, which financed development projects for under-privileged people all over the world. And between the foundation and her younger brother, Donald, her world was complete. She had no longer needed the kind of relationship we had had. And we had simply drifted apart.

But now it seemed as if she had come unglued. It either had something to do with the foundation or with her brother. I didn't have the faintest idea what I could do to help her with either.

I made it across town, over the Arlington Memorial Bridge, then down the Washington Parkway to the large hotel complex just across from the Pentagon, within half an hour. When I went inside, Pat Staley was waiting for me at the bar. She didn't see me at first, and I stood just within the doorway and watched her for a few seconds. She was still as beautiful as I remembered her, perhaps even a little more so, although her hair was done up in a bun, and she wore a very conservative business suit.

She spotted me when I was halfway across the bar, and she jumped off her stool, taking her drink, and met me, pecking me on the cheek.

"Thank God you've come," she said, looking around. "Let us sit over there," she said, motioning toward an empty booth near the rear of the room.

I guided her over, and when we were settled, and I had ordered a bourbon and water, she reached out for my hands, squeezing them hard.

"It's Don," she said. "He's gone."

"Your brother?" I asked.

She nodded shakily. "He's been gone for an entire month now, and I don't know what to do anymore."

"Gone where?"

"With that group. It's a religious cult. And Stewart called just this morning to tell me that Don had signed everything away. That's why I came down here. You have to help me. Please." She said all that in a breathless rush.

"Hold on a minute, Pat," I said. "You have to slow down. Start at the beginning, and tell me everything."

The cocktail waitress came with my drink, and when she was gone, I looked deeply into Pat's eyes.

"Now start at the beginning," I repeated.

She shook her head, looking away for a moment. "There isn't much for me to tell you, Nick," she said. "Because I simply don't know much of the story."

"Tell me what you know then," I said. "You asked for my help. Well I'm here now."

She nodded and took a sip of her drink. "About six months ago, Don met some people out on the west coast. He was looking into the conditions in the bario in Los Angeles for us."

"Don is working for the foundation now?" I asked.

"Yes. He graduated from college last year. Top

honors. According to our parents' will, when he graduated he was to be made a full director of the foundation."

"Go on," I prompted.

"Everything was fine for the first month or so after he got back from California, but then he started getting these weird telephone calls at all hours of the day and night."

"From who?"

"I don't know. I don't even know what they were all about. But Don became very secretive all of a sudden." She looked at me, and she seemed so helpless at that moment. "Don and I were always close, but suddenly he clammed up."

"Then what happened?"

"He took a trip out to Chicago, and ten days later, when he came back, he had totally changed. He was like a zombie."

"So what happened in Chicago?"

"I don't know. He just told me that he finally understood everything. But I had our attorney, Stewart Atterbury, hire someone to follow Don. And within a week the detectives reported back that Don had joined a religious cult whose headquarters are in Chicago. Something called The Church of the Final Reward."

"All right, so your brother finally got religion. What then?"

"He just got weirder and weirder. He wouldn't talk to me; he stopped doing all his work. And then . . ." she stopped a moment. "And then we think he started giving money to the crazy cult he had joined."

"His money, or the foundation's?"

"His money," she said, hanging her head. "But I

had to have Stewart check it out. I was frightened of what he had become."

"There's more?" I asked. "You said he had disappeared?"

She nodded, tears coming to her eyes now. "Four weeks ago he went to Chicago, and we haven't had a word from him since. No letters, no postcards, no phone calls, nothing."

"Did you try calling the church's headquarters."

"Yes, and they said they never heard of him." She opened her purse and withdrew a document. "Yesterday, Stewart got this in the mail. He showed it to me this morning."

I took the document and held it up to the light so that I could read it.

"It's legal," she said.

At first I couldn't quite make any sense of it, but finally I understood. It was a letter drawn up by Donald Staley, and signed by him, willing everything he owned to The Church of the Final Reward, on the event of his death.

When I was finished reading, I looked up at Pat, the tears were streaming down her cheeks. "You have to help me, Nick."

"How much of the foundation belongs to Donald?"

"I don't know. I guess around fifty million. But that's not it, Nick. I think those crazies out there in Chicago have brainwashed him into signing this, and now I think they plan to kill him."

TWO

I left Pat in her room at the motel around eleven-thirty, first making her promise me that she would remain there until morning. I didn't think this was going to turn out to be anything more than a younger brother going a little crazy. Yet when fifty million dollars was involved, anything could happen.

She had seemed a lot calmer than at dinner, and I told her that I would be back around eight in the morning to pick her up for breakfast, and then get her out to the airport. She was due back in New York by noon.

It was a Friday night, so there was a lot of traffic as I headed back into town, but I really didn't pay much attention to it, as I tried to piece together what little Pat had been able to tell me.

From what little I had known about Donald Staley, and from what Pat had added, it brought to mind the image of a very bright young man, with an even brighter future.

Pat had never really wanted to become involved in the Foundation. She had merely taken the job because there was no one else for it. Within a few

14

years, it had been her plan to let her brother take on more and more of the responsibilities.

She had wanted to move south somewhere. She had toyed with the idea of the Sarasota, Florida area. Perhaps she would choose one of the Keys, where she would settle down in a beachfront home and write, something she had always wanted to do.

The change she had described in her brother's behavior over the past months had come about too suddenly for me to believe it was merely another stage in his development.

Someone had meddled with Don's mind. There was little doubt about that. And there was even less doubt as to why they had done it. They wanted his money.

But, and it was a very large but, was the cult religion Don had become connected with ruthless enough to consider murder?

Fifty million dollars was at stake here. A tremendous amount of money. A fortune by any account. And money made people do extreme things. Murder among them.

I parked again in the basement garage beneath the Amalgamated Press and Wire Services Building, signed in with the night guard, and took the elevator up to the duty room.

Schmidt was there, briefing the mid-shift duty crew, and they all looked up as I came in.

"How was your date, Nick?" Schmidt quipped as I came across to him.

"Have you got something going tonight, Schmidty, or can you hang around awhile and give me a hand?"

The on-coming duty officer looked sharply at

me. "If this is official, Nick, we can handle it for you."

I shook my head. "Strictly personal for now, Peter."

Schmidt nodded. "I'll stick around for awhile," he said, and he followed me across to my office.

I took off my jacket, loosened my tie and rolled up my sleeves before I sat down behind my desk.

"Something wrong with Pat Staley?" Schmidt asked.

"With her brother," I said. "And for now I want this kept quiet. Just between you and me. If we come up with anything, anything at all tonight, I'll talk to Hawk about it in the morning."

"It's all right by me. What do you need help with?"

Quickly I told Schmidt everything I knew about Don Staley and the Staley Foundation, as well as what Pat had told me at the Marriott.

"The Church of the Final Reward," Schmidt said thoughtfully. "Something like the Moon cult? Or Jonestown?"

"I have no idea, but it's a possibility," I said. "Get yourself down to archives. I want a computer search on the church, especially its directors. Then you'd better dig out Pat Staley's file. She used to be a low-grade cryptographer here. There may be something in her jacket on her brother that came up on the background investigation."

"Anything else?"

"You'd better see if we have anything at all on the Staley Foundation, and exactly when and how Pat's parents were killed. It was an airplane accident a couple of years ago," I said. "Oh yes, and check to see if we have anything on the Foundation's attorney, Stewart Atterbury."

"I doubt if we're going to find much here or over at the agency," Schmidt said. "It sounds more like something the FBI would have."

"That's what I'm going to be doing. I have a friend over in the bureau. I'm going to roust him out, and see what he can come up with."

"All right," Schmidt said. "When I come up with anything, I'll pump it up here."

I was flipping through my telephone index as Schmidt was going out the door. Within a second or two I had found the number I was looking for, and I had the nightside operator dial it for me.

John Carver had been a young CIA officer in Korea during the conflict, and had remained in the Middle and Far East well into the sixties before he finally got out of the agency and went to work with the bureau.

I had first met him in Vietnam in 1964, and had worked with him again on an assignment in New York City in the mid-seventies.

The first time we had met, my cover was as a CIA operative. Carver had never learned any differently. He still believed I was with the company.

I had saved his life, through a chain of lucky circumstances, and he had never forgotten it. From time to time now we would have lunch and a couple of drinks together, and he always picked up the tab.

"If there's ever anything I can do for you, Nick, I want you to call me. Day or night. I mean it," he had told me on more than one occasion.

I was going to take him up on it now.

He answered his phone on the third ring.

"John, Nick Carter," I said.

"Nick, you old bastard, I was just thinking about you," Carver boomed. He was a large, boisterous man. "I was going to give you a ring in the next day or so to see if you wanted to get together for lunch."

"Possibly next week," I said. "But listen, John, I need a big favor."

"Now? Tonight?"

"If possible, John."

"Absolutely. What do you need?"

"I want you to go down to the bureau and look through your computer files for some information for me."

"Official or personal?" he asked, his voice guarded.

"Personal. But if you can't . . ."

"Bullshit," Carver said. "Tell me what you need, and you'll have it, if I can get to it."

Once again I repeated the story Pat had told me, ending up with the fact that I had someone helping with the records at this end.

"Sounds like something we might have, if they've done anything wrong," Carver said. "I'll be downtown within twenty minutes. Give me a couple of hours to run a preliminary search and I'll get back to you. Where can I reach you?"

I gave him my home phone number, and he agreed to call as soon as possible.

When we had hung up, I instructed our operator to monitor my home phone, and transfer any calls, in the blind, up here to my office.

I sat back for a moment then. I had set a couple

of wheels in motion. If there was any information to be had about The Church of the Final Reward, between Schmidt and Carver we would come up with it.

But after that, I was going to have to bring it to Hawk and get his blessings to continue. Although I technically was on vacation now, as a holder of the killmaster N3 designation, I was theoretically under constant control by AXE, and therefore David Hawk. Everything I said or did could possibly have an effect on the service and therefore on the United States.

After a while I went out into the duty room where I got myself a cup of coffee. Back in my office I had our operator check to see if there was a listing for the church in Chicago.

She called back a minute or two later with a telephone number and an address on the Loop, downtown Chicago.

Schmidt was the first in with his report, around three o'clock. He had pulled Pat Staley's file and had brought it with him, along with a single sheet of computer runoff.

He laid them both down on my desk. "There wasn't much here or over at the agency," he said.

"Give it to me from the top," I said.

"Pat Staley is clean. So is her brother, at least according to our files and Pat's background investigation. Their parents died in the crash of their Lear jet on takeoff from LaGuardia. National Transportation and Safety Board gave the incident a clean bill of health. Unforseen clear air turbulence. The pilot lost it and couldn't recover before they hit the ground."

"How about the church?" I asked.

"There's the printout," Schmidt said pointing to the sheet he had laid on my desk. "In 1974 they negotiated with the government of Brazil for the purchase of a fairly large tract of land, ten thousand acres, somewhere up the Amazon from the town of Manaus."

"And?" I prompted.

"And that's it, Nick. There was absolutely nothing else about the church, about Pat or her brother or their parents or the foundation or their attorney."

"You cross-indexed everything?"

"I checked and rechecked, Nick. Honestly, there is nothing else in our files, or the agency's files on any of this."

I had feared as much. "Thanks anyway, Schmidty."

"Anything else you need tonight?"

"Not a thing. Go on home to bed."

"Anything from the Bureau yet?"

I shook my head, and Schmidt got to his feet. "See you tomorrow?"

"Probably," I said absently, and I didn't hear Schmidt leave. What the hell did the church want with ten thousand acres of jungle along the Amazon? From what I could recall of my geography, Manaus had to be at least a thousand miles inland. Was it another Jonestown? And had Don been taken there?

Carver called half an hour later, apologizing for taking so much time and for coming back to me nearly empty handed.

"You had nothing on the church?" I asked.

"We did have a file, but from what I was told it was a very small one."

"Where is it now?"

"It's over at the Justice Department. Stewart Atterbury, the Staley Foundation's attorney, filed a complaint against the church over Donald Staley's will."

I hadn't thought of that possibility. Atterbury was just doing his job, trying to protect Don and the foundation, but I was going to have to tell Pat to call him off for the moment until I could look a little closer into this.

"Do you have any idea what the file contained, John?"

"No specifics. But it had something to do with a complaint lodged by the daughter of an elderly couple. In their eighties, from what I could gather. At any rate, it seems as if they joined the church, willed everything they owned to it, and then a month later committed suicide."

"Jesus," I swore half under my breath.

"Nick? Is it what you needed?"

"Just fine, John, just fine. I've got to run now, but I'll call you next week, and we can have lunch together. This time I'm going to buy."

"Sure thing . . ." Carver said, and I hung up.

Christ. The will first, and then suicide. The Church of the Final Reward.

Pat was definitely correct. Her brother was in danger. Very serious danger.

I grabbed my coat and left my office. Across the duty room I had the nightside officer book me on the ten-thirty A.M. flight from National Airport to Chicago's O'Hare, and told them to leave a message for Hawk that I would check in before I left, to explain everything.

Downstairs I got my car and drove quickly back across town to the Marriott. There was very little traffic at this time of night, and I made it there in something under fifteen minutes.

Fifty million dollars. The figure kept running through my head. A little old couple had committed suicide, willing everything they owned to the church. The daughter's objections had accomplished nothing.

If the church had been behind that, and had somehow caused the suicides, the church would certainly do everything within its power to get its hands on Donald Staley's fortune.

Killing him or forcing him into suicide was only a part of it. For that kind of money, I was sure that the church would allow no one to interfere. Certainly not his sister.

But little old couples, idealistic young men, and helpless women were one thing. I was something completely different.

Pat had evidently not been sleeping because she answered my knock almost immediately. When she was certain it was me, she opened the door and let me in.

"What is it?" she cried. "Did you find him?"

"Not yet, Pat, but you're going to pack your things and come with me now."

"What's wrong?" she said, alarmed.

"I'll explain on the way. Get dressed and get your things together. We're getting out of here."

She was wearing a nightgown, and she went into the bathroom, coming out a minute later dressed in slacks and a sweater. Together we threw her things in her suitcase and makeup bag, grabbed her coat, and went down to my car.

"What about my bill?"

"Send it to them," I said. "Your're staying at my place for the rest of the night."

"Why? What did you find out, Nick?"

I explained only part of what I had found out, leaving out the business about the old couple. But I told her that the church was probably looking for her right now. If and when they caught up with her, they would try to pressure her into calling off her investigation into her brother's disappearance.

"They'll do anything to protect their hold on Donald and his will," I told her. "For now I don't want you to do anything to force their hand."

"But I have to be back in New York by noon."

"And you will be," I said. "It's just that you'll stay the rest of the night at my place, and tomorrow you'll take a different flight on a different airline up to New York."

"But what about Don? What in God's name are they doing with him?"

"I'm going to find that out for you, but in the meantime, Pat, is there anyone you can stay with up in New York? I don't want you going to your apartment."

"Stewart . . ." she started to say.

"Not him," I said. "Anyone else?"

She shook her head. "There's no one."

"How soon will you be finished with your work?"

"Four maybe five o'clock."

"Fine, then I want you to come back down here.

Drive your own car. Stay at my apartment until I get back."

"Where are you going?"

"Chicago. But I'll be back later tonight, or Sunday at the latest."

She was worked up again, almost at wit's end. I reached out and caressed her cheek. "It'll all work out in the end, Pat, you'll see," I said with more conviction than I felt.

Don had been gone a month, and only two days ago his will came in the mail. They had presumably worked on him all that time. Even if I could get him away, I didn't know how much of him—the real Don Staley—would be left intact.

Pat was booked on a nine o'clock flight, and before I left I made sure she was in a cab heading for the airport. Then I went back to AXE headquarters, where I went directly up to Hawk's office on the fifth floor.

His secretary seemed harried, but when I came in, a look of relief flashed across her eyes.

"He's been waiting for you," she said. She buzzed Hawk. "Mr. Carter is here," she said.

"Send him in," Hawk's voice came over the intercom.

She buzzed the thickly padded door for me, and I went in, crossed the room and sat down in front of Hawk's desk.

He was a man in damn good shape with a thick shock of white hair. No one within AXE knew his correct age although guesses ranged from a low of the mid-fifties, to a high of the early eighties.

To me, David Hawk was ageless. He was just

Hawk. The hardbitten, cigar-smoking director of AXE, my boss, and the closest thing to being my father that he could be without actually being just that.

"Chicago is not exactly the best place this time of year for a vacation, Nick," he growled.

"No, sir," I said.

"All right, what the hell have you gotten yourself involved with now?" he said. He picked up a cigar and lit it, as I went through the entire story for the third time. This go around, however, I left absolutely nothing out. Including the fact that at one time Pat and I had had a relationship.

When I was finished, Hawk seemed to think a moment. "You think this kid is in danger?"

"Yes, sir," I said.

He thought a moment longer. "Should the agency become involved in this?"

"Not yet, sir. But I'll need some of our resources. If it turns out to be purely personal, I can reimburse the agency out of my own pocket."

"All right," he said. He sat forward. "I telephoned a friend over at the Justice Department this morning. He tells me they've started their own preliminary investigation into this church."

"Yes, sir," I said. "Stewart Atterbury contacted them."

"It's not Atterbury, although they have his complaint as well."

"Not Atterbury?"

"It's the Brazilian government. They're beginning to get worried about what's happening in their own jungles."

"Why don't they do something about it?"

"There's too much money involved, from what I was told," Hawk said. "The Church of the Final Reward has known assets in excess of one billion dollars in this country alone. They have more in Brazil."

"Good Lord," I said softly.

"Good Lord, exactly," Hawk said. "Religion, or at least this cult's brand of religion, is big business. And when that kind of money is involved, people who interfere can get hurt."

"Yes, sir."

"Be careful, Nick. Be very careful. Technically we have no business being in this investigation. Justice is handling it for now. But I'm giving you my go ahead on this. And you'll have AXE's backing. Unofficially, of course."

"Yes, sir," I said again, getting to my feet. "I leave for Chicago this morning."

"I know," Hawk said. "Good hunting."

"Thank you, sir," I said, and I headed toward the door, but Hawk stopped me.

"Thurmond said you handled yourself pretty well out there yesterday."

I didn't turn around. "Is he all right?"

"Mild concussion," Hawk said. "He'll be back to work within a week."

I couldn't believe it. "Yes . . ." I started to say, but Hawk interrupted me.

"We're setting him up down in Phoenix. He's going to be rewriting all our field-training manuals."

I turned around and looked at Hawk. There was a stern expression on his face.

"Good luck, Nicholas,"

I nodded and left his office.

THREE

My flight touched down at Chicago's O'Hare Airport a couple of minutes after noon. I had my overnight case sent over to the Airport Hyatt Regency Hotel, then had a quick sandwich at one of the terminal restaurants, and finally took a cab downtown.

The weather was cold and blustery, snow blowing down the long, traffic-clogged streets.

It was just one-thirty when the cabby dropped me off in front of a large building marked with nothing but the number 809 in large brass figures above the revolving doors.

The first floor was taken up with a bank of elevators and several dozen small shops, most of them selling religious books and items.

There were uniformed guards at the elevators and an information booth where many of the people coming and going stopped to get passes.

A pleasant young woman was seated at the booth and when I stepped up, she smiled.

"May I help you, sir?"

"I hope so," I said. "I was told that The Church of the Final Reward is headquartered in this building."

"Yes, sir?"

"I'd like to talk to a representative of the church, if you can direct me to the proper office."

"What is this in regard to, sir?" the woman asked.

"A friend of mine joined a few months ago, and I'm trying to locate him."

"I don't think there's anyone here who could help you . . ." she started.

"His name is Don Staley, and I've come from the Foundation with some new financial information. It's very important that I speak to someone who might know where he is."

A tall, distinguished looking, well-dressed man in his early fifties was just passing, and he stopped and came back to the booth.

"It's all right, Cindy," he said to the girl, and he turned to me. "You say you've come from the Staley Foundation?"

"Perhaps," I said. "It's very important that I get in contact with Don Staley. Financially very important. If you could be of some help?" I let it trail off.

"Be glad to do what I can for you, Mr. . . ?"

"Carter," I said. "Nick Carter." We shook hands.

"Michael Seidelman," he said. "Why don't you come up with me, and we'll see if we can do something for you, Mr. Carter."

I followed him through the gate and to one of the open elevators. As I passed the building directory, I glanced up at it. The only listings were for the first five floors, and all the names consisted of attorneys at law. There were no listings for any of the floors above the fifth, although this had to be at least a twenty-story building.

As the elevator doors closed, Seidelman inserted a key in a slot, twisted it to the right, and punched the button for the nineteenth floor. There were only two floors above that one.

When the elevator began to rise, he removed the key and looked at me and smiled.

"You say you work for the Staley Foundation?"

"Not exactly," I said. "I'm a friend of the family."

"Then you know Patricia," he said. "How is she doing these days?"

"Just fine. A little busy ever since Donald . . . ever since Donald decided to branch out on his own."

Seidelman said nothing else until we were deposited on the nineteenth floor.

The elevator opened onto a reception area. There was an older woman seated behind a huge desk and a wide carpeted corridor running to the left and right.

"Hold my calls for a bit, would you dear?" Seidelman told the woman. "And have Larry come down to my office if he's not tied up."

"Yes, Mr. Seidelman," the woman said.

I followed him to the left, down the corridor, and into a large, very plush office, dominated by a floor-to-ceiling glass wall that afforded a magnificent view of the city, and beyond to the east, Lake Michigan.

Seidelman was smiling. "On a clear day, during the summer, I spend entirely too much of my time watching the sailboat regattas out on the lake," he chuckled. "I swear, one of these days I'm going to have the window boarded up."

Someone knocked on the door.

"Come in," Seidelman called out.

Another tall, very distinguished looking man, impeccably dressed, stepped in. "You had a good trip, Michael?" he said.

"Excellent," Seidelman beamed. "Mr. Nick Carter here has come to talk with us about young Donald Staley. Mr. Carter is a friend of the Staley family."

"Larry Karsten," the man said, coming across the room and shaking my hand. "But I'm afraid we're not going to be of very much help to you." He glanced at Seidelman. "Have you explained to Mr. Carter yet?"

Seidelman shook his head. "I thought I'd let you explain everything to him. But Mr. Carter says he must get in contact with Donald. Something about a Foundation financial matter?" he asked, turning back to me.

"Don has been missing for the past month," I said ignoring the question. "His sister is frankly worried about him."

"Missing, you say?" Karsten said. "I can well understand why she would be upset. How can we help?"

"The Foundation's attorney, Mr. Atterbury, recently received a copy of Donald's will, leaving his fortune to your church."

Seidelman and Karsten both beamed. "It's wonderful," Karsten said.

"A magnificent gesture," Seidelman agreed.

"So we naturally assumed that you have been in

contact with Donald, and perhaps would know his whereabouts."

Seidelman started to say something but Karsten cut him off. "I'm terribly sorry, Mr. Carter, but none of us has seen Don in more than two weeks. From what I understood, he had returned to his home in New York City. But now you say he is missing. Very puzzling."

"Perhaps someone else on your staff might know where he went. Perhaps he made a friend or two while he was here?"

"He made many friends. Donald is a wonderfully bright young man."

"A heart as good as gold," Seidelman agreed. He took my elbow and guided me toward the door. "I'm sorry, Mr. Carter, that we could be of no help. But be sure to let us know when you find him."

I shrugged out of his light grasp. "Since both of you gentlemen know Donald so well, then perhaps you would like to testify at his competency hearing."

"What?" Karsten said sharply.

I smiled. "It was his parents' death, you see, that initially unhinged him. And then when he found out that his sister was a lesbian, it brought him to the edge, I'm afraid."

"Competency hearing, you say," Karsten mumbled.

"I'm afraid it's my fault," I said. "I saw the signs of his breakup three years ago. I discussed it with Stewart . . . Stewart Atterbury, the Foundation's attorney . . . as well as his sister. We've all agreed that Donald is just not responsible enough to manage his own fortune. It's been placed in trust until after his competency hearing. But if we can't find him . . ." I shook my head. "Well, I just don't know how the hearing could go in his favor if he's missing. I'm going to have to be honest with the court. I mean, we are talking about more than fifty million dollars here."

Both men were speechless.

I smiled again. "Please contact me through the Foundation if you should hear from Donald," I said, and I left the office, ambled nonchalantly down the corridor, nodded pleasantly at the receptionist and rang for the elevator.

It wouldn't take them very long to find out that I had been lying. Meanwhile, if they had plans of doing anything to Don, they would have to hold up. I was also hoping that since they now believed that I would present major testimony against Don at a competency hearing, they might even make a try on me.

If they did, it would certainly prove what I already suspected. Or at least it would prove it to me.

The elevator came and I stepped inside and punched the buttons for every floor from the eighteenth all the way down to the ground floor.

The doors closed, and the elevator started down, stopping at the eighteenth, the doors coming open onto a similar scene. A reception area, a woman seated behind a desk, corridors running right and left.

The woman looked up, startled. I smiled, shrugged, and the elevator doors closed and went down to the seventeenth.

This floor contained no reception room, just corridors running right and left. I held the doors open as I stepped halfway out and looked both ways down the corridors. Unmarked doors, nothing else.

Stepping back into the elevator, I let the doors close and went down to the sixteenth. This time when the doors opened, I was looking out across a large room filled with computers and terminals, dozens of people busy at work.

For several long seconds I stood there watching the activity until a large, burly man, his coat off, his tie loose, happened to look up and see me standing there.

"What the hell are you doing?" he shouted, and he started across the room toward me as the elevator doors closed, and I started down.

The fifteenth floor was another deserted corridor with unmarked doors. I stepped half out of the elevator, holding the door open with my right hand and looked both ways down the corridor. The elevator doors started to close even though I was holding the safety switch.

Someone had hit an override. Probably upstairs in the computer room.

If I remained on the elevator I would be stuck. I wanted them to come after me, but on my terms, and certainly not here in this building at this moment.

I quickly stepped off the elevator, the doors closed, and the elevator started down, not stopping at any of the floors I had punched buttons for.

Hurrying down the corridor to the left, I found the emergency stairwell and took the stairs down two at a time.

Once they discovered I had gotten off the elevator, they would be coming up the stairs for me.

I had just reached the eighth floor, when I heard a commotion far below. They were already starting up.

Making as little noise as I possibly could, I hurried down three more flights to the fifth floor, the others below me coming up fast.

Opening the exit door just a crack, I looked out into the corridor. Two men stood in front of an open office door at the far end of the corridor. They were talking and not looking in my direction.

I stepped into the corridor, making sure the door was closed, then catching my breath, strode purposefully down the corridor to the bank of elevators that came only as high as this floor.

The building directory in the lobby had listed the occupants of the first five floors as attorney's. Many of them, no doubt, worked for the church, but others were probably in private practice, only renting this space.

The two men looked up as I approached the elevators. I smiled and nodded, and they nodded back.

I punched the button for an elevator, and almost immediately one of the doors opened, several people got out, and I got in, hitting the button for the ground floor.

It only took a few seconds to reach the lobby, and when the elevator doors opened I tensed, ready to be challenged.

There were several men standing around the elevator that Seidelman and I had gone up in, and others at the end of the wide lobby corridor, standing at the stairwell door, but no one paid me the slightest attention as I crossed in front of the guards, passed the information booth, and then I was outside.

Dodging traffic, I hurried across the wide street, walked down about a half a block, and then stopped to look in a storefront window.

Every now and then I glanced across the street, and five minutes later a group of men emerged from the church's headquarters building. They looked around, then fanned out, three of them crossing the street.

They were after me. There was no doubt about it. And it was all I needed to know. The Church of the Final Reward wanted a fight with me, and they were going to get it.

I turned away from the window and headed down the street. At the corner I turned to the right and glanced back. There were two of them behind me. I hesitated for a couple of seconds, in plain view, and they spotted me and sped up.

I stepped around the corner and hurried down the block, looking for just the right place.

A block and a half later, with my two tails still a hundred yards behind me, I spotted an overfull parking lot tucked between two buildings across the street.

I had to wait for a couple of seconds for a break in traffic before I was able to get across, and the two men were almost on top of me by the time I reached the parking lot and threaded my way through the cars toward the back.

Tucked in one corner was a Volkswagen van. I

stepped around it, then spun around.

A couple of seconds later both men came around the rear of the van.

I stepped forward, driving my knee into the groin of the lead man, and as he went down, and the other one was reaching inside his coat, I hammered three quick rights to his face, and he went down as well.

No one on the street or in the parking lot attendant's booth had seen what had happened back here, and I quickly pulled the two men the rest of the way behind the van.

They were both armed with .38 snub-nosed revolvers, which I took and tossed under the next car over.

The one I had hit in the face was unconscious, but the one I had kneed was looking up at me with pure hate in his eyes.

"I don't like being followed," I said, as I flipped open his coat and reached for his wallet.

He tried to struggle up, and I hit his forehead with the heel of my hand, causing his head to bounce off the pavement.

His eyes glazed for a moment, and I took out his wallet. An identification card marked with THE CHURCH OF THE FINAL REWARD—SECURITY, identified him as Walter Fordham.

I took the card out and slipped it into my pocket, then tossed the wallet down on the pavement, and bent low over the man.

"I want you to listen to me very closely, Walter," I said.

He blinked but said nothing, nor did he make any move to struggle up again.

"Like I said before, I don't like being followed. You can tell your bosses that the next time they send someone after me, they won't be so lucky. The next time I won't just bust their balls. I'll break them into little pieces." I smiled and patted the man on the cheek. "You understand what I'm saying, Walter?"

The man nodded.

"Sometimes when I start working people over, I go a little crazy, you know? Sometimes I go too far.

I stood up and glanced out toward the street. We still hadn't attracted any attention.

When I looked back, Fordham was looking up at me, and his partner was starting to come around. "I hope to hell I don't run into you again, Walter. I hope not—for your sake."

I straightened my tie, stepped around the van, and left the parking lot.

Two blocks away I hailed a passing cab and directed the driver to take me out to the Hyatt Regency near the airport, then settled back for the twenty-minute ride through traffic.

The directors of the church had to be worried about me by now. Besides the story I had told them, they had caught me snooping around the building, and then I had beat up a couple of the goons they had sent out to bring me back.

Their next move, when it came, would be a little better thought out, and probably done with a lot more finesse.

I would have to be very careful from this moment on. I wasn't dealing with some five and dime outfit. The Church of the Final Reward's assets amounted to more than a billion dollars. In order to amass that kind of a fortune so quickly, and still attract as little attention as the church had, its directors had to be sharp, and certainly not used to anyone standing in their way.

At the hotel, which was just off the freeway by the airport, I signed in with the clerk, retrieved my overnight bag and went up to my room.

I changed shirts, and sportcoats, then retrieved my weapons from the specially designed radio-cassette player I use to get them through airport security measures.

The tiny, but effective, AXE-designed gas bomb in a special pouch high up on my inner thigh, my stiletto in its chamois sheath beneath my coat and strapped to my arm, and my 9 mm Luger in its shoulder holster on my left side, had been with me since the beginning. They were like old, trusted friends. Back at the church building I had felt almost naked without them. But then I hadn't really expected to run into so much trouble so soon.

It was just three P.M. here in Chicago, which meant it was four P.M. in New York. Before I had put Pat in the cab for the airport, I had promised to telephone her at the Foundation at five-thirty. She figured she would be done with her board meeting by then, and she wanted to know what I had found out before she headed back down to my apartment in Washington.

I left my room and went down to the hotel's cocktail lounge where I sat at the nearly-empty bar. After I had ordered myself a bourbon and water, I asked to use the bar phone. The barman set it up in front of me.

If someone from the church had already traced me out here, which was entirely possible considering their resources, I did not want them monitoring my telephone calls from my room, another distinct possibility.

When I had the outside operator, I placed a collect call to Amalgamated Press and Wire Services in Washington, D.C., giving a special code that would identify me to the AXE operator.

I got Hawk on the line almost immediately and explained everything that had happened so far.

"I'll contact Carver over at the Bureau for you and have him run down this Walter Fordham. They might have something on him for you," Hawk said.

"Thank you, sir," I said. "Meanwhile I'll need two other favors."

"Go ahead."

"First of all, see if you can contact someone in the Justice Department and get a complete copy of everything they have on the church, and if possible its directors, including Karsten and Seidelman. Also see what you can come up with on this piece of property they purchased in Brazil."

"That shouldn't be too terribly difficult, Nick, but from what I gather, no one has very much information on the church."

"Anything will help at this point, sir."

"The second favor?" he asked.

"It's Pat Staley. Have we anyone up in New York who could keep a loose watch on her?"

"Frankly no, Nick. Do you think she's in any danger?"

"She might be," I said.

Hawk was silent a moment. "I'll see what I can

do from this end," he said. "How long do you think you'll be staying in Chicago."

"Probably overnight. I'd like to take a closer look at that computer room."

"With care, Nicholas," Hawk cautioned. "And keep in touch."

"Yes, sir," I said, and I hung up.

I didn't think it would be too difficult to get into the building later tonight, probably sometime after midnight. They would have a pretty stiff security set up, I imagined, especially after my little jaunt through the floors this afternoon. But I've seen tougher setups before.

The barman came down to my end of the bar a few minutes later. "Are you Mr. Carter by any chance?" he asked.

"Who wants to know?" I asked.

"There is a message at the desk for you, sir," he said. "They tried your room but there was no answer. They checked here."

"Thanks," I said, and I picked up the phone and dialed for the desk. "Nick Carter," I said.

"Yes, sir," the operator said. "There is an urgent message that you immediately contact a Miss Pat Staley in New York." She gave me the number, and I asked her to ring it for me.

Something was wrong. She should have still been in her board meeting.

It seemed to take forever for the call to go through, and when it did, I had the Foundation's operator on the line.

"Pat Staley," I said. "Nick Carter calling."

"One moment, sir."

Pat was on the line a second later. "Nick? Is that you?" she shouted.

"It's me. What's wrong?"

"It's Don . . . oh God, it's Don. He called here twenty minutes ago. He sounded crazy. He said he was going to kill himself and that it was the only honorable thing for him to do."

"Calm down, Pat. Did he say where he was calling from?"

"No," she wailed.

"Was it long distance? Could you tell?"

"No . . . I don't know," she cried. "Wait. It was here in the city, I'm sure of it."

"Have you called his apartment?"

"There's no answer there," she said.

"His friends? A girl friend?"

"I don't know," she said. "I don't know any of his friends. He's got a girl friend, I think. Or at least he did."

"All right, listen to me. I want you to go over to his apartment right now, but take Stewart Atterbury with you. Get in there somehow and look through your brother's things. See if you can find anything that might indicate where he might have gone. Also look for an address book or a telephone index to see if you can find out who his friends are. Start calling around."

"What about you?" she asked.

"I'm on my way. I'll be in New York on the first plane. Just hang on, Pat. I'll be there."

FOUR

It was well after nine P.M. by the time I landed at LaGuardia and got my overnight bag from incoming luggage.

Up in the terminal I stopped at a pay phone and dialed Don Staley's number. It was answered on the first ring by a man.

"Hello?" he said guardedly.

"Stewart Atterbury?" I asked.

"Who's calling?"

"Nick Carter. Is Pat there?"

"This is Stewart Atterbury," he said. He sounded relieved. "Yes, Pat's right here. We've been waiting for you."

"Have you found Don?"

"No," Atterbury said. "We've gone through his apartment with a fine toothed comb. We found an address book, and we called all the names, but no one has seen or heard from him in the last four or five weeks."

"Were there any signs that he had been there at his apartment recently?"

"None that we could see," Atterbury said. "There was some stale food in the fridge, and half a loaf of moldy bread in the cupboard. I'd guess he hadn't been here in several weeks."

"How's Pat holding up?" I asked.

Atterbury hesitated a moment. "Not well," he said.

"Tell her we'll find her brother," I said. "I'll be there in twenty minutes."

"We'll be here," Atterbury said, and I hung up, crossed the terminal, and got a cab immediately.

I was tired. I hadn't slept the night before, nor had I been able to get much rest on the plane back to Washington, D.C. or up to New York. As the cab sped from LaGuardia Airport into the city and Don's apartment on Park Avenue South, I let my head rest back on the seat and closed my eyes.

Don had disappeared one month ago, and no one had heard a thing from him. I started poking around in Chicago, and suddenly he calls his sister and tells her he's going to commit suicide. It didn't really make much sense. Either the timing was coincidental, which I didn't believe was the case, or the Church of the Final Reward was more efficient than I had anticipated.

It was possible that they had somehow found out I was lying, and then had sent out the word for Don to die.

I didn't put any of that past them. But there was one major hitch to that line of thinking.

The church officials now knew that Don's will, leaving his fortune to the church, was being questioned. In the face of that it didn't make much sense that they would force his suicide. I would have thought it would have been a lot smarter of them to hold off for a while. Let the dust settle, and either arrange an accident for him, or make his suicide seem a little less forced.

Perhaps I was missing something. Some vital element that would explain it all. Riding into the city now, however, I couldn't think of a thing.

Atterbury cleared my entrance with the doorman on the ground floor, and he was waiting by Don's apartment door when I stepped off the elevator.

He was a small man, not over five-feet-five, very thin, with only whisps of white hair on his head, and thick, wire-rimmed glasses. He appeared to be in his late sixties or early seventies, and he looked haggard.

"I'm glad you could get here, Mr. Carter," he said shaking my hand and then leading me into the apartment.

"Still no word?" I asked.

"Not a thing."

Don's apartment was large and tastefully decorated. The stereo was playing softly, and only one light was on in the living room.

"Where's Pat?" I asked him.

"Sleeping," Atterbury said. "I had her doctor up here at around five. He gave her a powerful sedative. She should be out for awhile yet."

"Have you telephoned the police?"

Atterbury shook his head. "I wanted to, but Pat made me promise not to say anything to anyone until after you had arrived."

I went across the room, opened the drapes, then unlocked the balcony door and stepped outside.

It was just as cold here as it had been in Chicago.

Don's apartment was on the twenty-fifth floor, and far below the traffic was light. He could have committed suicide here.

Atterbury had come to the open door. "Can I offer you a drink, Mr. Carter?" he said.

"Bourbon and water," I said turning back. Something small and dark hanging from the back of the drape caught my eye and I stepped closer.

"What is it?" Atterbury asked.

I knew exactly what I was looking at. "Plenty of ice in that drink," I said, and then I motioned for him to keep quiet.

We both stepped back inside the apartment, and I motioned for him to go ahead and fix my drink. He gave me a strange look, then went across the room to the portable bar as I went to the far end of the drapes and carefully pulled back one edge.

A thin wire led down the back of the drapes from the tiny microphone and disappeared into the thick carpeting.

Following the baseboard around the room, I came to a telephone jack. Coming up from the carpet, and leading into the terminal, was the thin wire.

Someone had bugged Don's apartment.

Atterbury had mixed my drink, and I went across to him and took it. "This room is bugged," I whispered close to him. He flinched. "I'm going to leave, but I'll be right back. Don't say anything."

His eyes were wide, but he nodded.

I took a deep drink of the bourbon, then set the glass down, crossed the apartment and softly let myself out.

At the elevator I punched the button for the basement, and on the way down I pulled out my Luger, levered a round into the chamber, and stuffed the gun in my jacket pocket.

The bug could have been placed in Don's apartment months ago. But simply hiding the microphone on the back of the drapes was sloppy. The church did not use amateurs, or at least I didn't think they would, which meant that the bugging operation had been a hurry-up job. Like sometime this afternoon before Pat and Atterbury showed up. And probably in direct reaction to my snooping around in Chicago.

The elevator doors opened on the basement storage area, mostly empty except for a few crates to the left.

The lights toward the rear of the huge area were out, and as I started forward, I pulled out my Luger and snapped the safety off.

I angled off to the right out of the illuminated area, and then very carefully followed the concrete wall back.

The electric and telephone service entered the building from the floor, near the back of the main room.

I pocketed my Luger, pulled out my penlight and shined it up on the large telephone terminal cabinet. It was locked, of course, but it didn't matter. Just barely visible, along a seam in the concrete, a thin wire emerged from the terminal cabinet and disappeared through the back wall.

Unless I had been specifically looking for it, I would have never spotted the wire. Although it had been hastily installed, it was well done.

I clicked my penlight off, and once again pulled out my Luger as I followed the back wall away from the terminal cabinet, coming finally to a steel door.

I put my ear to it. There was the sound of machinery running on the other side. The room probably contained the heating plant for the building.

Softly, I opened the door a crack, and immediately I could smell cigarette smoke. Someone was seated at a small table to the right, earphones on his head, hunched over a tape recorder.

I yanked the door all the way open and stepped inside, bringing my Luger up.

The man half turned, and when he saw me just inside the door, he reached out toward his equipment, and the lights went out.

I leaped to the left, crouching down, and a second later the man fired two shots in my direction, the bullets whining off the metal door.

Crawling on my hands and knees, I scrambled behind the heating equipment. A third shot ricochetted off the machinery just above my head.

And then the room was still, except for the sounds of the heating equipment. Across the room I could see a dim light coming from an indicator dial on the tape recorder.

Whoever had bugged Don's apartment did not want this confrontation, I was certain of it. But he would not leave without the tape recorder.

I continued to watch the light. But then it went out, or was blocked!

I fired three shots in quick succession, one directly where the light had been, one to the left and the last to the right.

The man cried out and then crashed to the floor.

I leaped up and was across the room in a couple of strides, my Luger in my right hand and my penlight in my left. I flicked on the light.

One of my shots had caught him in the right shoulder; the other had blown the back of his head off.

I holstered my Luger and quickly went through his pockets, coming up with a wallet that contained a security identification card from the Church of the Final Reward. His name had been Robert Biggs, and he had a New York address.

For a moment I stared at the card. *A New York address!* That meant the church probably had offices here in the city.

Christ! I slipped the ID card out of the man's wallet, then replaced the wallet in his pocket. Next I grabbed the tape recorder, ripping the wire out of the wall, and left the furnace room, racing across to the elevator.

The elevator car had not gone up, and the door opened as soon as I punched the button.

Atterbury answered the apartment door on my first knock, and when I came in with the tape recorder he looked incredulous.

"Where did you find that?" he asked, following me into the living room where I set the machine down on the coffee table.

"In the basement," I said. "Call the information operator and ask for the telephone number and address of the Church of the Final Reward's office here in New York."

"They have an office here?"

"Yes," I snapped. "Now hurry!"

While Atterbury was talking on the phone, I plugged the tape recorder in, rewound all the tape onto one spool, then took it off the machine and put it in my overnight bag.

He was just hanging up when I finished. And I looked up.

"Anything?"

"They have offices in the World Trade Center. But how did you know that?"

"I didn't," I said. "Call the number. I'll get Pat out of bed." I had a feeling that whatever was going to happen with Don, was going to happen tonight. And I knew where it was going to happen, even though it still didn't make any sense to me. It was just too sloppy.

Pat was lying, fully clothed, on the bed, a light cover thrown over her. I sat her up.

"Come on, Pat, wake up. It's me, Nick. Time to wake up."

She opened her eyes and looked up at me. "Nick?" she said thickly.

I pulled the cover back and undressed her.

"Nick?" she said, and she started to giggle.

When I had her clothes off, I carried her into the bathroom, and while I propped her up in the shower, I turned on the cold water.

For just an instant, as the spray hit her, she didn't react, but then she reared back with a shriek.

"What . . . God . . . What are you doing?" she sputtered, trying to fight her way out of the tub. But I held her there for several moments longer, until finally I shut the water off and helped her out.

As I was drying her off, she put her arms around me.

"Nick?" she said. "Nick? Make love to me. Nicky, please."

"Later, Pat. But now you've got to wake up. I think I know where Don is. But you're going to have to help."

"Don?" she mumbled. "Donny? You've found Donny?"

"I think so," I said, tossing the towel aside.

Back in the bedroom I helped her get dressed, and she gradually became more awake.

"You said you found Donny?" she asked.

"I think so," I said.

Atterbury came in, his face white. "There are police there. A police officer answered the telephone."

"Jesus," I swore. "Is Don there?"

"I didn't ask," Atterbury said. "I just hung up."

"Is your car downstairs?"

"In the garage," he said.

"Go down and get it right now. Pull around to the front. We'll meet you there."

"Donny?" Pat mumbled.

"Move it!" I shouted.

Atterbury jerked as if he had been slapped. He turned and raced out of the room. I heard him go out the door, and then I turned and finished dressing Pat.

I walked her into the living room where I grabbed her coat and put it on her. And then propping her up by the door, I pulled on my coat, grabbed my overnight case, and we left the apartment, taking the elevator down to the lobby.

Atterbury was just pulling up in his Lincoln Continental as Pat and I emerged from the building, and he helped me get her in the front seat. I climbed in next to her, and Atterbury got back in behind the wheel.

For a moment he just sat there.

"Let's go," I shouted.

He looked at me, confused. "Where?"

"Jesus. The World Trade Center!" I couldn't believe it.

Atterbury pulled slowly away from the curb and we headed downtown. There was something wrong with the man, but I suppose I was too preoccupied to really notice it. His complexion was definitely pale, and there was a line of sweat on his upper lip.

All the way downtown, Pat kept mumbling about her brother, but she wasn't making much sense. I was almost certain now that the church had been keeping Don at its headquarters here in New York for at least the past couple of weeks, working on him all the while. They had finally gotten him to the point where he had made out his will, and now he was going to commit suicide.

The cops being at the church's offices in the World Trade Center clinched it for me. I only hoped that we weren't too late.

The street in front of the World Trade Center twin towers was cordoned off when we arrived. There were police everywhere, and as we came up to the barriers, one of the traffic cops waved us along.

Atterbury stopped the car and I jumped out. "What's going on in there, officer?" I asked.

"Just move it along, will you?" the cop said, tiredly.

"I have reason to believe that someone in there is

attempting to commit suicide. I have his sister with me," I said.

The cop stiffened, then looked over at the car. "I'll tell them you're coming," he said, making his decision. "They're on the eightieth floor in the north tower. But you better hurry, he's put a desk through the window and he's standing halfway through the hole."

I jumped back in the car as the traffic cops were moving the barriers aside. "Let's go. It's the north tower."

We pulled through the barriers and continued down the street. "He's here?" Atterbury asked. "They said he was here?"

"The eightieth floor."

"Donny?" Pat asked, sitting up. She was starting to come around.

Atterbury pulled up in front of the building, and I helped Pat out of the car, across the walk and through the front door. There were a dozen cops in the lobby by the elevators.

A plain clothes cop broke away from the group and hurried across to us. "Are you the ones related to the guy on eighty?"

"This is his sister," I said.

"Let's go, let's go," he said hustling us to a waiting elevator. We all stepped aboard the car; the doors slid shut and we started up.

"How did you know he was here?" the cop asked.

"It's a long story, which we'll tell you when this is over with," I said.

The cop's eyes narrowed, and then he glanced at Pat. "What's the matter with the sister?"

"Sleeping pills," I said. "She's not awake yet."

We made it to the eightieth floor in something under a minute, and the detective hustled us down a long corridor and through an unmarked door that led to a huge suite of offices that were jammed now with people.

"Is this them?" another plain clothes cop asked, coming away from one of the inner doors.

"Is Donny here?" Pat cried out.

"Donald Staley?" the detective asked.

"That's him," I said. "What's the situation in there?"

"He came up here earlier this evening, threatened some people here with a gun, then shoved a desk out the window. He's hanging half in and half out right now, threatening to jump."

"How about getting a rope on him from above?"

The cop shook his head. "Too much wind up there tonight. And two people have already died trying to stop this character."

"Who?" I asked.

"A couple of people from the church that use these offices. They tried to grab him, and they went out the window with the desk. Another one of them is in there now with our negotiator trying to talk him back."

Pat had listened to all this wide eyed, and she pulled away from me, stepped around the detective and went into the office.

"Donny?" she cried.

I was right behind her.

Don Staley was sitting on the floor of the large office, one leg inside, and the other dangling over the edge where the window had been. His hands were bloody from where he had been hanging onto the shards of glass. The wind outside moaned at the opening.

"Donny?" Pat cried again. She stepped past the two men who had been talking with him.

"Don't come any closer," Don screamed.

"It's me," Pat said. "Don, don't you recognize me?" She continued toward him.

"No!" Don shrieked, and he rolled outward, shoving himself away with his hands, and he was gone.

"Don!" Pat screamed, and she leaped toward the open window.

I was right after her, and just managed to grab her at the last possible second and dragged her farther back into the room. I didn't know if she would have jumped after her brother, or if she even knew what she was doing at that moment.

She screamed his name again, and then collapsed in my arms sobbing as I led her out of the office.

Atterbury was standing there, staring wide eyed at us. He was shaking.

The detective who had brought us up here, and the one who had been here, came out of the office shaking their heads.

I passed Pat over to Atterbury, "Get her back to her own apartment, Stewart."

"No," she cried. "I don't want to be alone, Nick. Come with me please."

"I'll be there in a little while, Pat. Go ahead with Stewart."

"Promise?" she said.

"I'll be there in just a little while," I said to her. "Stay with her until I get there, will you, Stewart?"

Atterbury nodded.

"Hold up there," one of the detectives said.

"I'll give you everything you'll need," I said.

The cop turned on me. "She's his sister, so just who the hell are you?"

"Nick Carter," I said. "A friend of the family. I work with Amalgamated Press and Wire Services out of Washington, D.C., and I've been tracking Donald Staley for some time now."

"Tracking him?"

"That's right. He's been missing for nearly a month. He willed his fortune—fifty million—to this church. And now he's dead. Right here from the church's offices."

The church official who had been inside trying to talk Don out of jumping, glared at me, pure hate in his eyes. But he said nothing.

The detective whistled. "All right, no one leaves these offices until we get this story straight. And I mean no one."

FIVE

A cold wind blew up the grassy slopes of the St. Bernadette Cemetary on Long Island as the minister was saying the final words for Donald Staley.

There were only a dozen people at the funeral besides Pat, Stewart Atterbury and myself, but among them was Michael Seidelman from The Church of the Final Reward's Chicago headquarters.

He stood across the open grave from us, and every now and then our eyes met. He was crying.

Don had leaped to his death three nights ago, and the past seventy-two hours had been strange, almost unreal. But the events of those three days had proved beyond a doubt that the church had destroyed Don, and that it was far more powerful than any of us had ever imagined. So powerful, in fact, that absolutely nothing had come of Donald's death.

The church had been held totally blameless. Don had been a basically unstable character, the coroner's jury had ruled. The pressures of modern society had led him to seek comfort within the church. But it had been too little too late.

His will, according to Atterbury, would be challenged, but he had admitted privately to me that absolutely nothing would come of it. The church would get his fortune.

Pat looked up at me, tears in her eyes, and I put my arm around her shoulder and drew her a little closer.

That night, after Don had killed himself, had been a nightmare for her.

We had been questioned at the World Trade Center for nearly two hours. During that time Pat had let it slip that I was something more than just a simple newsman from a wire service, and before I could do a thing about it, I was searched.

A few eyebrows had risen when they came up with my Luger, but the reaction had been hostile when they found my stiletto.

One of the detectives had drawn his service revolver and pointed it at me. "Jesus H. Christ, we've got ourselves a walking arsenal here," he said. "Cuff all three of them."

"You're making a mistake," I said, as the handcuffs were being snapped on.

"We'll see about that downtown," the detective had snapped, and we were taken directly to headquarters where we were separated.

I was fingerprinted and photographed, and then strip-searched, both detectives nearly going through the ceiling when my gas bomb was found.

"Do I get to make my one telephone call?" I asked. This was going to have to be stopped before it went too much farther.

"I'm inclined to say no," the cop said sharply,

"but I'm curious as hell to find out who you're going to call."

Still handcuffed, I was taken back upstairs to one of the interrogation rooms where I was sat down at a small table and given the use of a telephone.

One of the detectives sat across from me with a monitor earphone in one ear, and the other one stood near the door watching me.

I dialed our Washington crises number, identified myself, and Hawk was on the line, his tone guarded. The number I had called, and the procedure I had used, told him that I was in some kind of serious trouble.

"Good evening, Nicholas," Hawk said. "Where are you calling from?"

"Police headquarters in New York City. I'm under arrest for carrying three illegal weapons, and possibly for complicity in the death of Donald Staley. I was at his apartment with Pat and the Foundation's attorney, Stewart Atterbury. Did anyone try to reach Pat there?"

"Yes, a friend of ours did. He was a little late, but he did take care of everything."

I breathed a sigh of relief. Hawk had managed to get someone up here to New York after all, and he evidently found the mess I had left in the basement heating plant room and had taken care of it.

"Thank you, sir," I said, and I hung up.

The detective across the table from me was startled, and he opened his mouth to speak, but at first nothing came out.

"May I have a cigarette while we wait?" I asked pleasantly.

"What the hell was that all about?" the cop sputtered, but then he turned to his partner. "Get someone over to the Staley kid's apartment on the double. Something is going on there."

I sat forward. "I'd wait on that one, for just a few minutes," I said.

"What are you trying to pull, Carter, whoever the hell you are?" the detective shouted.

"Staley was murdered," I said softly. "And I'm trying to prove it."

"Bullshit! I saw him take a nose dive out the window myself."

"The Church of the Final Reward is a cult religion. They had control of Donald Staley for more than a month, during which time they brainwashed him into jumping out the window."

"Why would they do something like that?"

"Because Staley was a very rich young man. He willed everything he owned to the church. And I've got a hunch that they've done the same thing before with other people."

Both detectives stared at me for several seconds until the one by the door came back to the table.

"You say you're a reporter with a wire service. Why the fancy weapons?"

"I can't tell you that now," I said. "But within a minute or so, someone will be walking through that door with an explanation."

"I guess we'll just call your bluff, Carter," the cop said. He turned to his partner. "I'll get his prints down to the FBI. They should be able to come up with a make on him."

The door opened at that moment, and a tall, husky man in a captain's uniform came in, followed by another man in civilian clothes.

"Captain Parker," the detective seated across

from me said, jumping up.

"You're Nick Carter?" Parker asked.

I nodded.

"Get the cuffs off him," he snapped. One of the detectives complied. "Mr. Carter, here, works for the government. Is there anything we can do for you?"

I got to my feet. The detectives were staring open-mouthed at me. "I want Miss Staley and Mr. Atterbury released and all records of this entire action yanked from your files and destroyed."

The captain was nodding.

"For now, this never happened. Staley jumped to his death, and that's the end of that as far as this department is concerned."

"Yes, sir," the captain said.

"Sorry," the detectives both mumbled.

I smiled. "Don't worry about it. You were just doing your jobs. Now I want you to forget this ever happened."

They nodded.

An hour later our clothing had been returned to us, I had my weapons and my overnight bag back, and Atterbury drove us uptown to Pat's apartment where he dropped us off.

"They're going to be coming after his money now," he said.

"See what you can do to stop it," I said. "Or at least hold it up in court for as long as you can."

"Are you going after them?"

I nodded. "You're damned right I'm going after them. They killed Don, and they tried to get to me."

He looked at Pat, who was in a daze, shook his head, and then drove off.

I took Pat up to her apartment, put her in the bathtub, then, while she was soaking, fixed us something to eat.

She came out into the kitchen wearing a terrycloth bathrobe and a towel around her hair just as I was laying out the food on the counter. She seemed much more awake, more herself now.

"Just like old times," she said, sitting up on one of the stools.

"Coffee or brandy?" I asked.

"Both," she said.

I poured a couple of cups of coffee, adding brandy to both, then brought them over to the counter where I sat down across from her.

She cradled her cup in both hands and carefully sipped at the hot brew. She was shaking.

"Why Donny?" she said after a moment. "Why'd they have to pick him, Nick?"

"His money," I said.

She nodded. "It was a stupid question." She carefully set her cup down and then shoved her plate aside.

"You should eat something, Pat."

"The bastards," she said, the tears streaming down her cheeks. "The dirty bastards."

I came around the counter, and she broke down sobbing in my arms.

"Oh God, Nick, what am I going to do?"

I helped her off the stool and led her back to her bedroom, where I threw the covers back on her bed and laid her down.

As I started to straighten up, she grabbed my arm and pulled me back. "Don't go, please don't go. Stay here with me tonight."

"I'll just be in the living room."

"No. I mean right here, Nick. In bed with me. I need you tonight. I need you to make love to me."

"Pat . . ."

"Please. I've never needed anyone more than I need you right now."

I reached down and kissed her deeply on the lips, her arms around my neck, and she drew me down on top of her.

"Nicholas . . . oh God, Nicholas," she cried softly.

When we parted, I got up, took off my clothes, then came back to bed with her and helped her take off her robe. We made love wildly and passionately, her long legs wrapped around my body.

The next day I had remained in New York to help Pat with the funeral arrangements for her brother.

The day before, after first making sure that one of our people would stick around to keep a very tight watch on her, I had flown down to Washington, where I spent the day at AXE headquarters.

Hawk had opened a file on the Church of The Final Reward, making it a legitimate assignment for me.

"The Brazilian government has asked for our help in this," he explained to me. "Unofficially, of course, but they want to know whether or not the church is legitimate. They don't want another Jonestown on their hands down there."

But despite a full day's work, using all the resources of AXE, and therefore the CIA and FBI, I was able to come up with very little else on the church.

It was listed as a nonprofit organization, its

funds being used entirely for the ministry. Spreading the word.

The only thing I did learn was that the church's founder and guiding spirit was a man by the name of Franklin Knox. There was no file on him with the bureau, and about all anyone knew was that he had been born somewhere in Georgia, sometime in the thirties, and had been a bible salesman until the late sixties or early seventies when he had founded his church in Atlanta. In 1972 he had moved his operations up to Chicago.

I had returned to New York this morning, where I had helped Pat and Atterbury with the final arrangements, and now it was finished.

"Ashes to ashes, dust to dust," the minister intoned, "we commend the soul of Donald Stearns Staley to his maker, for life everlasting. Amen."

He sprinkled holy water on the open grave, then on the casket, bowed his head for several long seconds, and then came around to us.

"Miss Staley," he said. "There is hope for all of us. You must understand that Donald is in a far happier place now. He is at peace at last."

Pat was just nodding; she could not speak.

When the minister left, the other people came up one by one, to offer their condolences, and I broke away from them and went around the open grave to where Seidelman was standing, hands together, head bowed.

When I approached, he looked up. "Mr. Carter, isn't it?"

"That's right," I said.

"A tragedy. A terrible tragedy," he said. "He was so young and innocent."

"Probably the only truthful words you've spoken," I said sharply. I reached in my coat pocket and pulled out the identification cards I had taken from Fordham in Chicago, and from the man whom I had killed in the basement of Donald's apartment building. I handed them over to him. "I believe these belong to you," I said.

He took them from me, his eyes narrowing, and put them in his pocket. "Leave well enough alone," he said softly, menacingly.

"I wonder what would happen if I took out my gun and shot you dead here and now," I said.

He took a step backwards.

"Have you willed your worldly goods to the church, Mr. Seidelman?"

"Of course," he said.

"Then let me suggest you always keep a close watch over your shoulder. You can never tell who might be gaining on you." I turned and went back to Pat and Atterbury and walked with them back down the hill to the limousine.

"Who was that you were talking with?" Atterbury asked.

"No one important," I said.

"I see," Atterbury said, glancing back at Seidelman who was still standing by Donald's grave.

We got in the limousine which took us farther out on the Island to Atterbury's home near Hampton Bays.

The afternoon went slowly. Many of Pat's friends, and people from the Foundation who had not attended the funeral, showed up to offer their condolences.

The three of us had dinner alone around six-thirty P.M., and then Pat and I left in her car around eight for the eighty mile drive back into the city.

I was leaving in the morning, and Pat wanted to spend this last night alone with me. Three other people from AXE would be coming up in the morning to keep a very close watch on Pat here in New York while I was gone, so I wasn't too worried about her. I didn't think the church would try anything against her anyway. Not this soon. And they had no grudge against her in any event. It was me they wanted. Especially after my little exchange with Seidelman this afternoon.

It was late, sometime after two in the morning, when I woke up aware of the fact that, for some reason, we were no longer alone in the apartment.

Pat was cradled in my left arm, her lovely breasts crushed against my chest, her long legs intertwined with mine.

We had come back to her apartment early, had finished a bottle of very good Dom Perignon, and then had gone to bed where we had made slow, gentle love to the strains of Tchaikovsky's violin concerto.

We had fallen asleep in each other's arms, able at least for that moment to forget the danger we were both in, able for that moment to forget the terrible image of her brother leaping to his death from the eightieth floor of the World Trade Center.

Now they were back to finish what they had begun, and lying naked here, I felt more vulnerable than ever.

Slowly, so as to make absolutely no noise, I moved myself away from Pat, disengaging my legs from her and easing my arm from beneath her head.

Whoever was in the apartment with us was somewhere directly across the room. I could hear breathing and some other soft, scratching noise.

Every muscle in my body tensed as I made ready to fling back the covers and leap up, but at that moment a blinding light flashed in the corner, the sudden sharp odor of sulphur wafted across to me, and something very sharp pierced my neck just above my right shoulder.

"Nick?" Pat screamed as I leaped out of the bed and stumbled to the floor as the covers twisted around my legs.

A heavy, numb feeling began to spread rapidly from my neck, down my shoulder, and through my right side. I struggled to get up.

Flames suddenly sprung to life from a pile of clothing and paper in the corner, and somehow I managed to get unsteadily to my feet.

Two men were at the door; both of them were tall and husky.

"He's up," one of them shouted, his voice coming from a long way off.

"Never mind, Sid, let's get out of here," the other one said.

Sid. The name and the face swam around in my fuzzy brain as I took several shaky steps forward, finally collapsing near the chair where I had tossed my clothes and my Luger in its shoulder holster.

I was fumbling for it when something slammed into my face, snapping my head back, and I fell over.

The man named Sid was standing over me, his face garishly illuminated in the flames that were rapidly filling the apartment.

"Die, pig," he said, and he laughed.

Through my haze, I heard the bedroom door slam and then the door out into the corridor.

The bedroom was filled with choking smoke, and it seemed to be spinning as I rolled over and crawled back to the bed.

Pat's bare arm was hanging over the edge of the bed. I grabbed it and pulled, rolling her off the bed and on top of me on the floor.

She was only semi-conscious and couldn't help me at all as I crawled, pulling her across the bedroom to the door. I couldn't catch my breath, and my heart was pounding nearly out of my chest as I reached up with fumbling hands for the doorknob, found it, and turned it.

The door came open, and I was able to pull Pat out of the bedroom and into the large living room, where I stood up. I half carried and half dragged her to the front door and out into the corridor.

Stumbling back into the apartment, I managed to grab the telephone just inside the door and dial the operator.

It was hard for me to make myself understood. It seemed as if my tongue was too big for my mouth, and I kept fumbling with the words.

But then she understood that there was a fire, and somehow I gave her the address.

Smoke was pouring out of the bedroom now, and flames were shooting out along the ceiling.

I dropped the phone and went back out into the corridor where I managed to drag Pat another twenty feet down the corridor, until I could not go any farther, and I collapsed in a heap, the building spinning, my head pounding.

SIX

I was vaguely aware that someone had come into the corridor and was helping me to my feet, but I was too far gone to know who it was or even care.

There were stairs, and then for a few brief moments I was intensely cold, until I was lying on something soft, a blanket thrown over me.

It was quiet then for a long time, until the cold came again, and Pat was lying next to me beneath the blanket, and we were moving.

I was sure I heard sirens, and once I heard a horn, but I was drifting, and although I heard these things they meant nothing to me.

It was morning. The sun streamed through tall windows across the room from the four poster bed that I was lying in.

For several minutes I was content to lie where I was, warm and comfortable. But then a vision of the fire and of the two men in Pat's apartment came back to me in a rush, and I sat up with a start, my head pounding.

Painfully I flipped back the covers and got out of the bed. For a second or two I had to stand where I was until the room stopped spinning, but then I stumbled across to a chair where clothing was laid out for me.

Stewart Atterbury came in just as I was pulling on a shirt. He seemed agitated.

"Thank God you're awake," he said, rushing across the room to me.

"Where's Pat?"

"In the next room. She's all right. But she hasn't come around yet."

"What the hell happened, Stewart?" I asked. "How'd we get here?"

"Some man came by with you. You were both nude. We carried you in and put you to bed."

"Who was he?"

"He had a FBI identification. Said you were to call your office as soon as you came around." Atterbury looked at me. "He said you and Pat had both been drugged. He said something about a fire."

It must have been one of our people. The goons that Seidelman had sent after us could have easily gotten around him to us. Evidently he had spotted the fire and had gotten us out of there.

"What happened? Was it the church?"

"You're damned right it was the church. They tried to kill us last night."

"Good Lord," Atterbury said, backing up a step. "Good Lord," he said again.

I was through playing games with these people. If there had been even the slightest doubt lingering at the back of my mind, it was completely gone now.

"Is there a telephone here?" I asked looking around.

"On the desk," Atterbury said at the same moment I spotted it and went across the room.

"Can Pat stay here for a few days?" I asked.

"Of course," Atterbury said. "As long as she wants."

"She may not want to stay here at all, but I want you to keep her here until I return. Force her to stay if you have to."

"Where are you going?"

"That doesn't matter," I said. "I just have to know that Pat will remain here."

"She will. I'll see to it," Atterbury said.

"Now if you'll leave me for a moment, I have a call to make."

"Of course," Atterbury said, and he left the room.

I dialed our Washington number and within a few seconds I had Hawk on the line and explained everything that had happened to us, including the exchange between Seidelman and myself at Don's funeral.

"I just now heard about it," Hawk said. "Are you and Miss Staley all right?"

"Aside from a headache, I'm fine," I said. "Pat is still out."

"They're playing rough."

"Yes, sir. Now it's time for us to return the favor."

"What have you got in mind, Nick?"

"I'm going to pay another visit to church headquarters out in Chicago. An unannounced visit. I want to see what their computer has to say about all this. Should be interesting."

"Do you want the Bureau in on this?"

"No," I said. "But you're going to have to side-track any investigation here into the cause of the fire. I want it kept quiet, at least for now."

"They're not too happy with us in New York City since your arrest, but it can be done without too much fuss."

I still had my watch. It read a few minutes after eight A.M. "Have someone meet me at the Pan Am ticket counter at LaGuardia with replacement weapons for me. Mine were lost in the fire."

"I can have someone there by noon," Hawk said.

"I'll need some clothes, money and a class IV equipment inventory."

"All right," Hawk said. "How about Miss Staley?"

"She'll be staying here until I return. She'll be all right, I think. I doubt if they'll try anything out here."

"We can have someone posted if need be."

"Probably not necessary, sir," I said. "I still think they're after me and not Pat. Once I get out of here she'll be okay."

"All right," Hawk said after a slight pause. "Let's not underestimate these people any longer, Nick. Be careful."

"Yes, sir," I said.

After I hung up, I went into the bathroom, took a quick shower, shaved with the things there, then got dressed again.

Pat was sleeping soundly when I checked on her, and without disturbing her I backed out of the room, softly closed the door and went downstairs.

Atterbury was waiting for me in the dining room

with coffee and breakfast. He was dressed and ready to leave for work.

"What staff have you got out here?" I asked as I sat down at the table.

He poured me a cup of coffee and handed it across. "A cook, housekeeper, and a groundsman outside."

"No one else?"

He shook his head.

"Do you trust them?"

"They've been with me for years. Of course I trust them."

"Fine," I said sipping the coffee. "Where'd these clothes I'm wearing come from?"

Atterbury hung his head. "They were Donald's. He and Pat came out here often. They both maintain wardrobes here."

"I see," I said. "I'm going to ride back into town with you this morning. I'll return the clothes later.

Atterbury waved it off. "Are you returning to Washington?"

"Not immediately," I said. "There are a couple of things I have to look into first."

"What about the fire investigation? If we could prove that the church tried to kill you and Patricia, it might help open up a line of questioning about Donald's suicide."

"There'll be no fire investigation. At least none for the moment. I just want you to continue doing everything you can to stall the proceedings over Don's will."

Atterbury shrugged. "That could be stalled for months. Perhaps even a year or more."

"All I need is a few days," I said.

Atterbury looked sharply at me. "What *are* you going to do?"

"Just a little investigative reporting," I said.

He started to say something, but then clamped it off.

After we ate breakfast, I checked on Pat again. She was still sleeping peacefully. Then I went outside and got in the car with Atterbury. Immediately his chauffeur pulled away from the house and headed into Manhattan.

"Where do you want to be dropped off, Nick?" Atterbury asked after we had ridden in silence for a few minutes.

"Anywhere uptown," I said absently. I was thinking at that moment of the blank look on Donald Staley's face just before he leapt to his death. It was a look so totally devoid of real human emotion, that at that moment he could have been nothing more than a department store manikin. It was an impression that would remain with me for a very long time to come, made more harsh by the fact that the church had produced that effect in him.

Atterbury dropped me off at Fifty-Seventh and Fifth a few minutes after ten A.M.

"Don't say anything about Pat's whereabouts to anyone at the Foundation," I said, standing by the open door.

Atterbury looked startled. "Do you think someone at the Foundation will tell the church of her whereabouts?"

"It's possible," I said. "Just don't say anything to anyone, at least for the time being."

"Whatever you say, Nick," Atterbury said, troubled.

I closed the door and watched until the limousine was out of sight; then I hailed a cab, instructing the driver to take me out to LaGuardia Airport.

All the way out to the airport, I kept glancing over my shoulder out the rear window, but as far as I could tell I wasn't being followed.

At the airport I entered the terminal at the American Airlines area, then walked back up to the Pan Am ticket area and took a seat where I could watch the counter, the front doors, and the main corridor.

The church had made a couple of mistakes with me. This time they would be on their toes. So would I. But I didn't think they'd expect me to show up in Chicago. Not this soon, and not alone.

For the next hour or so I watched the airline passengers coming and going through the terminal, and as far as I could tell no one was paying much attention to me.

About one minute before noon, a tall, black man, carrying a suitcase and an overnight bag, came down the corridor, turned into the Pan Am terminal area and stopped.

He spotted me almost immediately, and he came over, set the bags down, then turned and walked off.

I waited for another ten minutes, then nonchalantly got up, picked up the bags, and left the Pan Am area, entering one of the small cocktail lounges halfway across the terminal.

I sat down at one of the tables, bought myself a

bourbon and water, and then opened the overnight case. Right on top were my airline tickets on Republic, leaving for Chicago at one-thirty P.M., and beneath that was a large portable radio/cassette player which contained, I knew, my weapons.

An envelope with the tickets contained a number of credit cards in my own name, and several hundred dollars in cash, as well as a battered wallet.

I pocketed the tickets, the wallet and the money, leisurely finished my drink, then went over to the Republic Airlines gate area. I went through the security check and then walked down to the gate to wait for my flight.

It was ten below zero, and a raw wind was blowing when we landed at O'Hare. I retrieved my suitcase and took a shuttle bus over to the Airport Hyatt Regency where I checked in, and was given a room on the fifth floor.

I quickly showered, shaved again, and changed into my own clothes, strapping on my weapons.

AXE's equipment specialists had packed a civilian parka for me, along with the gear I had requested, anticipating that I might have to spend some time outside in this weather.

I stuffed the few pieces of equipment in the inner and outer pockets of the coat, then left my room, setting up a telltale high on the door, near the hinge, so that if anyone entered my room while I was gone, I would know about it.

I went downstairs and had a quick bite to eat in the dining room, then took a cab downtown, cruising slowly past the church's headquarters building before instructing the cabby to drop me off two blocks later.

I paid him, then headed back on foot.

As I had remembered from the last time here, the building next to the church's was a seven story department store. The two buildings abutted each other, and if I could get to the roof of the department store, without being detected, sometime after dark, I figured I had a very good chance of getting into the church's building without tripping any alarms.

I hurried past the church building, averting my face so that there would be no chance of me being spotted and recognized if someone was posted at the front doors, then went into the department store.

A sign on a metal rack just inside the front doors listed the store's hours: *Open nine A.M. to five-thirty P.M.*

It was just four-thirty now, which gave me an hour to get in place before the last few shoppers left.

The department store was busy with shoppers, as I threaded my way toward the elevators at the back of the building.

Only the first five floors were open to the public. The sixth and seventh contained offices.

I rode the elevator up to the fifth floor, which was not quite as busy as the ground floor, and when I was reasonably certain that no one was paying me any attention, I slipped out the exit door to the stairwell.

A small glass window was set in the steel door just about eye height, and I looked through it waiting to see if anyone had spotted me and was coming to investigate.

But after a minute or two when no one came, I

turned and hurried up the stairs to the sixth floor where I looked through the window into a large, open room filled with dozens of people busy at desks.

Continuing up to the seventh floor, I again glanced through the window. This floor contained a plushly carpeted corridor, with paintings hanging on the walls. The executive suite.

About twenty feet down the corridor a man stood waiting for the elevator. The doors opened, and he stepped on and was gone.

The stairs continued up, ending at a windowless steel door with an alarmed trip lock. The door would open, but when it did an alarm would sound throughout the building, unless the trip lock was deactivated with a key.

Quickly I slipped out my stiletto, and getting down on my knees, I began working on the lock. It was a fairly simple cylinder type, and within a half a minute I had the five pins depressed, and the plug turned.

I straightened up, leaving the stiletto in the lock, and pushed the locking bar forward. It stuck for a moment, but then popped open with a loud snap, and the door swung open.

The alarm did not sound. I stepped half outside into the intensely cold, biting wind, and looked across the roof at the church's building which rose another fourteen stories.

It was already starting to get dark out, and most of the windows in the church building were lit up. From where I stood I could even see people seated at desks a few floors up.

If I was spotted coming out of the stairwell, there was a possibility that fact might be mentioned to someone. But there was no other way. I could not remain there in the stairwell until everyone next door had gone for the night. The department store night guards would be almost certain to check this door.

Back inside, with the door still open, I reset the locking bar, checked to make sure there wasn't a secondary alarm trip on the latch itself in the door frame, and then reset the alarm switch, removing my stiletto from the lock.

Still no alarm sounded, and a moment later I had slipped outside and had carefully reclosed the door.

No matter what happened now, I would not be able to return the same way I had come. There was no way of deactivating the alarm from outside, nor was there any simple way of opening the door.

Keeping low, and in the shadows as much as possible, I hurried across the roof to the air conditioning units housed in their own utility room. The door lock was another simple cylinder lock, and I had it opened in less than a minute and slipped inside, closing the door behind me.

Two huge air conditioning units filled most of the space inside. On three walls were louvered vents which hinged outwards, and by inserting my stiletto in one of the slots and pushing all the way out, I could just look outside and see a few floors of the church building to the left, and the exit door of the department store to my right.

I wedged the blade in place so that the vent remained open, then stepped back away from the opening and lit myself a cigarette.

All that had taken me only fifteen minutes, so it

was still not even five o'clock yet. The store closed at five-thirty, and it would be at least an hour after that before the night watchmen over there finished their initial rounds and settled down for the night with their first cup of coffee.

There was no telling, however, just how long the church employees would remain in their offices, although I suspected most of them would be quitting and gone for the night no later than six.

I would have to give it several more hours, just to make sure that no stragglers remained behind. Sometime between nine and ten, I figured. Four to five hours from now. It was going to be a long, cold wait up here in this unheated building.

A few minutes after six the department store exit door opened, and an older man in a dark uniform, carrying a flashlight and a large ring of keys, stepped halfway out onto the roof.

He shined his light around, flashed it past the air conditioning building where I was watching from, shivered, and then went back inside, closing the door after him.

About the same time, the lights in the church building began going out, starting mostly with the lower floors, the pattern gradually working itself upwards as the higher ranking executives finished their last minute work for the day.

The windows on the sixteenth floor, which contained the computer room, were blocked off, so there was no way of telling from here what was happening up there. It was a safe bet, however, that the lights were never turned out on that floor. The computers would be running twenty-four hours a day, hopefully with only a skeleton crew at night.

By eight-thirty, all the lights, except for a few windows on the top floor, had been turned off. And by nine-thirty, even those last few windows went dark, and I got ready to go to work.

I was freezing, so that when I retrieved my stiletto and stepped out onto the roof, the bitterly cold wind that was blowing didn't seem much worse than inside.

I quickly crossed the department store roof to the side of the church building. The eighth floor windows were about five feet above the level of the roof on which I stood, and I peered through one of them into a small office that contained two desks. A map of the west coast, from California all the way up to Alaska, was pinned to the wall, markers at various cities, with a large cluster of colored pins in and around the Los Angeles area.

Glancing over my shoulder to make sure no one was at the department store exit door, I pulled the glass cutter and putty I had been supplied with out of my parka pocket and set to work cutting a fist-sized hole in the window just above the latch.

Before I had cut a complete circle, I laid a thick strip of putty on the glass, then finished with the cutter.

The section broke away cleanly, with only a small cracking noise, and I pulled it out with the putty attached.

As far as I could tell, the window was not wired, and within seconds I unsnapped the latch, raised the window, and climbed inside.

I reclosed the window, scraped the putty off the small, circular piece of glass, then ran a narrow bead of putty around the edge, and carefully stuck the glass back in place before closing the curtains.

There would be no telltale cold breeze coming through the hole in the window for someone to discover if they opened this door.

At the office door, I put my ear to the wood, but there were no sounds from the corridor, and I opened the door a crack.

The corridor was deserted. I slipped out of the office and hurried down to the stairwell door and started up, taking the stairs two at a time.

At the sixteenth floor I stopped and put my ear to the metal door. Faintly I could hear the sounds of people talking and of machinery running.

I inspected the hinge line of the door with my penlight, and near the top I could see that it was insulated from the metal frame. This door was alarmed, as I had expected it would be. But there were people talking on the other side. Several people.

This wasn't going to be as easy as I had first hoped it would be. But still not impossible.

I turned away from the door and continued up the stairs where at the nineteenth floor I slipped the simple catch latch with one of my credit cards and stepped into the carpeted corridor.

The lighting was subdued and the floor apparently deserted. I hurried down the corridor to the secretary's desk just across from the elevator.

The indicator above the door showed that the car was down on the ground floor. And keeping one eye on it, I sat down at the secretary's desk and opened drawers until I found what I was looking for, the building's telephone directory.

There was no listing under computer or terminal, but under the listing, records, there were several names and three digit telephone numbers, among them a number for George Stevenson, second shift duty operator.

I cleared my throat, then picked up the telephone and dialed the number.

It was answered on the third ring. "Records," a man said.

"That you Stevenson?" I said, and I coughed.

"This is Stevenson."

"Larry and I have a bit of a problem up here. Come on up right away, and bring the operational manual with you."

"Yes, sir," Stevenson said, hesitating. "Ah . . . who is this?"

"You idiot," I snapped. "This is Seidelman," I coughed again.

"Sorry, sir, didn't recognize your voice with your cold. Be right up."

I hung up the phone, unzippered my parka, and pulled out my Luger.

From this point on, there would be no doubt in anyone's mind what I was up to here. And after tonight a multi-national corporation's assets would be brought to bear in an effort to stop me.

It wasn't going to be a picnic, but Seidelman, Karsten and the head of the entire show, the Reverend Franklin Knox, were going to be in for a few surprises.

SEVEN

A few minutes later the elevator started up from the first floor, stopping for about ten seconds at the sixteenth, before continuing up.

I got up and stepped farther back into the secretary's alcove, so that I was standing in the shadows just behind a couple of filing cabinets.

The elevator door opened, and a tall, rotund man who had to weigh at least three hundred pounds stepped off and turned down the corridor.

I waited until the elevator doors closed before I stepped out from behind the file cabinets.

"George," I called softly.

The man was halfway down the corridor, and he spun on his heel and started back before he realized that something was wrong. He stopped in his tracks.

I raised my Luger. "Come on, George. I won't hurt you if you cooperate with me."

"Who the hell are you . . ." he started to say, but then recognition dawned in his eyes. "You," he hissed.

The word had evidently gotten around. "That's right," I said, smiling. "So you know I'll kill you

83

unless you do exactly as I tell you." That was a bluff. I had no intention of killing this man; what was happening here with the church wasn't his fault, as far as I knew.

"What do you want?"

"Come on down here and let's take a look at that operational manual."

At first he didn't move. But then I reached up with my left hand and snapped a round into the Luger's firing chamber, the noise loud in the quiet corridor, and he came the rest of the way.

I stepped aside, closer to the elevator.

"Put the book down on the desk and open it to data recall."

"What level?" he asked automatically.

"I want a membership list."

He blanched. "That could take some time. There's tens of thousands of members."

"I want the real membership list, George," I said. "You know the one I'm talking about."

He started to shake his head, but I motioned him toward the desk with the Luger. He moved over and set the book down.

"I want a list of members who've already signed wills leaving what they own to the church."

"What are you talking about?" he said. He seemed sincere.

I glanced over my shoulder at the elevator indicator. The car was still here on the nineteenth floor. "Who else is down in records at this moment?"

"No one," he said. This time he was obviously lying. I could see it in his eyes.

"I heard other people talking, George. Who else is down there?"

"Two operators," he said. "Both of them key punch girls."

"No security people?"

He shook his head. "They're down on six and up on twenty-one . . ." he started, but then he realized his error.

I reached behind me and punched the elevator button. The door opened immediately.

"Bring the book, we're going downstairs," I said, backing into the elevator and holding the door with my free hand.

Stevenson hesitated a moment.

"Let's go, George, I'm beginning to run out of patience with you, and we've still got a lot to do."

He gathered up the book and slowly came forward, stepping into the elevator as I backed up. He hit the button for the sixteenth floor, and we started down.

"There *are* some people . . . good people . . . who've made out their wills to the church. But I can tell you right now, there aren't very many of them."

"Fine," I said. "Then it shouldn't take us very long."

The elevator door opened on the computer room, and we stepped off.

A young woman was seated at a key punch machine a few feet away. She glanced up, and then did a double take, her mouth opening to say something.

"Up off that chair," I said softly. "Now!"

She saw my gun, her eyes went wide, and she got up.

"Where's the other one?" I snapped.

"I don't know," Stevenson said.

"Cindy had to go to the bathroom," the woman said. "She'll be right back."

Another young woman appeared from the back of the room and came toward us. She could see that I was here, but she apparently could not tell that something was wrong. She was smiling.

"Come on over here, Cindy," I called to her.

She looked puzzled, but she came the rest of the way, finally spotting my gun, and she stopped, her right hand coming to her mouth.

"Anyone else on this floor?"

The first girl shook her head.

"Fine," I said. "Now I want you all to listen very carefully. If you all do *exactly* as I tell you, no one will get hurt, and I'll be gone as soon as I get what I came for."

"Oh God," Cindy whimpered.

"The main terminal is over this way," Stevenson said, motioning toward the center of the room. "But you're on a wild goose chase."

"We'll let the computer tell me that," I said. "All right, let's get started."

The two women preceded Stevenson and me around several rows of data punch units to a semi-circular grouping of equipment that was obviously the computer's main terminal and control center. There were half a dozen tape and disk memory drives to one side, a key punch card sorter and a hard copy printer to the other.

I motioned for the women to have a seat in the center of the area, away from the controls.

"Either of you moves from your chair, or you make any motion whatsoever to sound an alarm, and I will shoot George here first," I said.

They hastily pulled chairs over and sat down,

their hands folded in their laps.

"Now, George, I want you to open the operational manual to the data search and recall section," I said. "I wouldn't want you to push the wrong buttons."

He did as I asked, laying the book on the console, then moving away from it to the terminal control keyboard.

"I won't do anything to alert our security people," Stevenson said. "I want you to believe that."

"I want to believe it, George. All I want is my list, with addresses, and then I'll be off."

I glanced at the recall instructions, which were laid out in tabular form indicating the sequence of keys to punch for a desired output.

When I looked up, Stevenson had already brought up the query circuit, the words: STAND-BY FOR PROGRAMMING DATA appearing on the wide CRT display.

He looked over at me. "Can I go ahead?"

I nodded.

His fingers flashed over the keyboard, the CRT coming to life.

```
        OPEN
        SEARCH AND RECALL
        DISPLAY HARD COPY
        MEMBERSHIP LIST
        SUB CLASS—MEMBERSHIP,
        LIVE, WILLS TO
        COTFR.
        ANNOTATED SUB-LIST—
        PROVIDING CURRENT
        ADDRESSES.
        START
```

* * *

A red light winked on the top of the terminal and Stevenson seemed startled.

"What is it?" I asked softly.

"I don't know yet," he said shaking his head. He punched a number of other keys in rapid succession, and the red light went out.

RESTRICTED DATA
IDENTIFY

He reached for the keyboard.

"Hold it," I snapped.

He looked up.

"That will be information you'd not have access to," I said. "Have you got a personal identifier, or is that accomplished within the computer by name only?"

"Personal identifier," Stevenson said.

"Do you know Seidelman's code?"

George shook his head, but one of the girls sat forward. "I do," she said.

"Give it to George then. Seidelman is going to request the list," I said.

Stevenson punched the seven unit alpha-numeric code into the machine, and moments later the hard copy printer began spitting out names and addresses.

At first George just idly watched the machine, but as it gradually became evident that even this sub-list was going to be long, his eyes widened.

"What the hell . . ." he started.

"Think about it, George," I said stepping closer to the printer.

He looked up.

"You have Seidelman's identifier. After I'm gone, ask the computer to tell you the names of the church members who have already died and left their money to the church. The list will be long."

He was shaking his head. "There's something wrong here. There has to be some kind of a mistake."

"There's a mistake, all right. And I'm trying to fix it."

The wide computer paper, filled with names and addresses, came out of the printer sheet after sheet, folding itself into a hopper.

It took nearly twenty minutes before the machine finally fell silent. George wound the last sheet out of the printer, then pulled the stack out of the hopper. It was at least four inches thick.

"There has to be a couple of thousand names here," he said in awe.

"That's right, George. And I'll tell you something else. Everyone on that list is in mortal danger right now."

"From what?" he asked innocently.

"From the church," I said. "Now put the list down on the console, and step away from it."

He shook his head and backed up. I was afraid of that. I did not want to hurt him, but I'd have to if there was no other way.

"I sincerely don't want to hurt you," I said.

"Give him the list," Cindy said. George looked at her. "If what he says is true, then he can help. If it's not true, then giving him the list won't hurt a thing."

Stevenson stood there indecisively for several

seconds, until finally he set the list down on the computer console, then stepped back away from it.

I grabbed the bulky list, folded it over as best I could and stuffed it inside my parka.

"We're going down the stairs, together."

"Where are you taking us?" Cindy asked, frightened.

"Just halfway down, and then I'll let you three come back up here. By the time you'd be able to get to a phone and sound the alarm, I'll be long gone," I said. "I haven't hurt you so far. I won't now, if you cooperate with me just a little longer. Then you can do whatever you want."

The girls got up from their chairs. George nodded his assent, and we all crossed the computer terminal room, entered the stairwell, and started down.

Our footsteps echoed hollowly as we descended from the sixteenth floor, but no one said a thing until we reached the eighth.

"Hold up here," I said.

Stevenson and the women stopped and looked at me.

"You three can go back up now. I go down the rest of the way by myself."

Without a word, they turned around and started back up. At the first landing Stevenson looked back down at me, shook his head, and then disappeared from view.

I remained on the eighth floor landing for a couple of minutes listening to them, and then I opened the stairwell door and stepped into the corridor.

I hurried down to the office I had entered the

building from, slipped inside, and threw the curtains back.

The window opened easily, and I slipped outside, jumping lightly to the roof of the department store five feet below.

Turning back and reaching up, I closed the window and then raced across the roof. As I ran I reached inside my parka and withdrew the coil of thin, but incredibly strong nylon line, and friction shackles AXE had supplied in my entry and search kit.

At the rear of the building there was a three-foot lip. I looked over the edge. Below was the department store's loading dock, a snow clogged alley running both ways to the streets.

I tied one end of the line in a large loop and brought it back to the vent pipe, looping it over the cap so that it could not slide up and off.

Back at the edge, I looked over once again. The loading dock was lit by a night light, but there was no activity down there, seventy feet below.

I flipped the free end of the line over the edge, attached the friction shackles, and was about to swing my legs over the edge when a shot ricocheted off the brickwork inches away.

Spinning around, I dropped low and to the left as I grabbed my Luger which I had stuffed in a parka pocket.

A second shot was fired, going high and to the right, the flash coming from a window far above on the twenty-first floor.

I scrambled back to the right as a third shot rang out, and I fired four shots in quick succession, at least one of them breaking the window pane above where the flash had come from.

I had just run out of time. Stevenson and the girls had evidently used a phone just a few floors up from me, and the security people, knowing what I was probably going to do, were trying to pin me down here until they could get someone below.

I fired two more shots at the window, then grabbed the friction shackles and literally jumped over the edge, a near miss from above plucking at my parka sleeve.

The shackles brought me up short about ten feet down, the sudden shock nearly pulling my shoulders out of joint. But then I was sliding down the line in a rapid but controlled descent, using my feet and legs as shock absorbers against the side of the building.

Down on the loading dock, I released the line, leaped down to the alley, and headed in a dead run toward the street.

At the corner a half a dozen shots were fired at me from the rear of the church building, but then I was out on the street.

I skipped quickly to the other side, raced to the end of the block, skidded around the corner, and a half a block later managed to grab a cab, directing him to take me out to the Airport Hyatt Regency on the double.

"Well, you're sure dressed for this weather," the cabby said, conversationally.

"You bet," I replied looking over my shoulder. Three burly men had just come around the corner, and they stopped, looking directly at me in the cab.

Within five minutes they'd be on their way out to the airport, expecting I'd be going there in an attempt to escape. It wouldn't take them very long to discover that I was staying at the Hyatt. It was going to be tight.

The cabby talked to me about the weather all the way out to the hotel. When he dropped me off, I tossed a twenty dollar bill over the seat, told him to keep the change, and hurried into the hotel, taking the elevator immediately up to the fifth floor.

My little telltale on the door was still in place, and I went into my room, grabbed my overnight case and suitcase, and went back down to the lobby where I paid my bill and hurried out the back way through the restaurant.

O'Hare Airport would be out. They'd be waiting there for me. And although I figured I would be able to fight my way out of almost anything they threw at me, I didn't want to take the risk of an innocent bystander getting in the line of fire.

I walked around the back of the building to where the driveway out front curved around and merged with the highway.

From here I could see the front entrance to the hotel. A cab had just pulled up and discharged four large men in topcoats. They hurried into the hotel, and the cab started my way. Empty.

I stepped out from the side of the building and flagged him down. Tossing my bags in the back seat, I climbed in.

"Where to, buddy?" the cabby asked, pulling away from the curb.

"Milwaukee," I said.

"Milwaukee?" the cabby asked, looking at me in the rear view mirror. "That'll cost you sixty bucks."

"Fine," I said. I pulled a hundred dollar bill out of my pocket and handed it over to him. "I don't want to take all night."

"Yes, sir," he said, straightening up in his seat, and we shot out onto the freeway and headed north for the fifty-mile drive.

I stayed the night at the Marc Plaza downtown, and in the morning took the first flight out to New York City, arriving a little after eleven A.M.

I telephoned Hawk in Washington from the airport and told him what had happened in Chicago, and about the list I had brought back with me.

During the flight I had looked through some of the many pages of names and addresses. The heaviest concentrations were women, most of them on the east and west coasts, as well as a few bigger cities in the midwest, such as Chicago, St. Louis, and Kansas City.

"It amounts to a death list," I told Hawk.

"We'll turn it over to the Bureau as soon as you get back," he said.

"I'm going out to pick up Pat now," I said. "We'll be driving down to Washington this afternoon."

"I see," Hawk said.

"I'll want her put up in a safehouse somewhere, until this blows over."

"Of course, Nick. But what about the church itself?"

I was suddenly tired of the entire affair. I had come up with the hit list, something the Bureau could not have done on its own. It would be up to them now to talk to each of the several thousand people and gather enough evidence to prove that the church was indeed trying to brainwash them into not only leaving their money to the church, but into ultimately committing suicide.

"There should be enough in this list to bring to the Justice Department," I said. "They won't cover this up."

"Fine," Hawk said. "It looks as if I'll have another assignment for you within a few days in any event. Once you get back, you can get started on your briefing."

"Anything you can tell me right now?"

"No, but you'll need your tuxedo."

"Yes, sir," I said, and I hung up.

I rented a car at the Avis counter, and twenty minutes later I was heading east through Queens toward Atterbury's home near Hampton Bays.

EIGHT

All the way out to Long Island, I kept thinking about Pat and how I was going to explain to her that I was passing the investigation of the church and of her brother's death over to the FBI.

She wasn't going to take it very well. When she had come to me in Washington and asked for my help, I had promised her that everything would work out all right.

The opposite had happened so far. Her brother was dead. She and I had almost been killed. And the church continued to operate.

I shook my head in exasperation. This had all been so crazy. So meaningless. The church, as it turned out, was nothing more than a cleverly conceived scam to bilk innocent people out of their life savings. Seidelman, Karsten, and the others like them, were nothing more than high class con men who worked under the guise of their religion.

It definitely was not a job for AXE, although I did wonder what the hell the church used all its money for.

A light snow had begun to fall by the time I turned off the highway and continued down the long gravel driveway into Atterbury's home. The trees were bare, and with the snow and wind, the place seemed isolated, and deserted.

I didn't plan on remaining here for the night on the off chance that the church would somehow trace me here and try something. Parking the car in front, I went up on the wide porch and rang the bell.

Atterbury's housekeeper answered the door a minute later, and she let me in, although she seemed somewhat surprised to see me.

"Is Mr. Atterbury here?" I asked.

"No, sir," the woman said. "He telephoned last night to say that he would be staying in town for the rest of the week."

That was odd, I thought. He had promised me that he would keep an eye on Pat.

"May I tell Mr. Atterbury that you stopped by to see him, sir?" the woman asked.

"No, that's all right. I'll give him a call when I get back to the city. I just came out to pick up Miss Staley."

"You just missed her," the housekeeper said.

"What?" I snapped, grabbing the startled woman.

She hiccoughed. "Patricia left here about eleven-thirty with the two fellows that Mr. Atterbury sent out for her."

"Who were they?"

"I don't know," the frightened woman sputtered. "They were from the Foundation, I think."

"Did Mr. Atterbury tell you he was sending someone for Pat?"

"No, he didn't. But that nice Mr. Barnes telephoned the Foundation and let me speak with one of the directors. He said it was all right."

I tried to think. "How long were they here?"

"They showed up early, about eight o'clock I think it was, and they had breakfast with Patricia before they went into the study."

"Did they say where they were going?"

"Why, yes," the housekeeper said. "They told me that they were flying down to Washington to meet with you and Mr. Atterbury. That's why I was so surprised to see you here."

They had her. Christ, they had her. I released the woman. "Can I use a telephone?"

"Yes, sir," she said, and she showed me into the study.

When she was gone, I telephoned Hawk and explained what had happened out here, asking him to check with the airlines at LaGuardia and Kennedy and call me back here when he found out something.

Next, I telephoned the Staley Foundation, the operator answering on the second ring.

"Stewart Atterbury, please," I said. "Nick Carter calling."

"I'm sorry, Mr. Carter. Mr. Atterbury is out of the office."

"When do you expect him back?"

"I really couldn't say, sir. He left for Washington, D.C. about two hours ago."

I stood there a long moment, the telephone to my ear, unable to say a thing. Atterbury had remained in town overnight, leaving Pat out here alone. And then this morning he had left. I didn't want it to make any sense, but I was getting a very strong gut feeling that Atterbury was something other than he seemed to be

"Thanks," I finally mumbled, and I hung up and sat down on the edge of the desk. I lit myself a cigarette, inhaling deeply.

It would do absolutely no good for me to run off half cocked now. They were all gone, and until Hawk got back to me with some concrete information, I'd get no where by leaving here. But I had a hunch I knew exactly where they had gone.

After awhile I went around behind the desk and began looking through the drawers. There was little other than the usual things found in desk drawers, except in one which contained a Smith & Wesson .38 police special, with a box of shells. The pistol was loaded.

Atterbury's telephone index and appointments book contained nothing other than Foundation business as far as I could tell. But if Atterbury was connected in some fashion with the Church of the Final Reward, I didn't think he'd leave anything incriminating lying around.

The telephone rang a few minutes later, and I picked it up. "Yes?"

"I have some bad news for you, Nick," Hawk said.

"I can guess."

"Miss Staley, Stewart Atterbury, Robert Barnes and Howard Stenger left Kennedy at noon for Bogota, Columbia."

"Damn," I swore. I was afraid of that. "Have we anyone down there who can intercept them at the airport? I don't believe that's their final destination."

"We could get someone there in time," Hawk said. "But our relations with Columbia are so strained now, an incident at the airport . . . if one came up . . . would be disastrous."

"Yes, sir," I said. "I'm coming in. I'll leave for the airport immediately. In the meantime, see if you can come up with any IDs on Barnes and Stenger."

"They're both employees of the church," Hawk said several hours later. I was seated across from him in his office.

"That nails it," I said. "They'll be taking Pat down to Brazil. Manaus, first, and then from there to the church's holding farther up the Amazon. Do we know its exact location?"

"I did some more checking this afternoon, Nick, and I'm afraid there's more bad news."

I waited.

"The Brazilian government has withdrawn its complaint against the church. One of their people from their embassy stopped by at the State Department earlier this morning and told them that it had all been an unfortunate mistake."

"Money talks," I said morosely.

"It gets worse," Hawk said. "The embassy spokesman told our people that his government would look dimly on any efforts by us to in any way interfere with the lawful business of its citizens."

"What?"

"The Reverend Franklin Knox, it seems, has suddenly become a Brazilian citizen."

"We can't just let this slide, sir," I said.

"Of course not," Hawk pressed a button on his desk console.

"Do we know where the church's holding is located?"

"Not exactly," Hawk said. "As far as anyone knows it's located up the Amazon from Manaus. Evidently somewhere in the vicinity of a river town called Coari."

"They're ready for him now, sir," Hawk's secretary said over the intercom.

"He's on his way down," Hawk spoke into his desk unit. "I assumed that you would want to follow this up."

I nodded. "When do I leave?"

"First thing in the morning. An Ozark flight to Miami, then Pan Am to Caracas. I thought it would be best to keep you away from Bogota. From Caracas you're booked on a Varig Airlines feeder flight directly into Manaus."

"If Knox has become a Brazilian citizen, the church will probably have Manaus pretty well tied up. I'll need a cover."

"They're waiting for you downstairs. You'll be Roland Cartier, a French diamond dealer working out of Amsterdam and New York City. There've been persistent rumors of large diamond finds farther up the Amazon and Negro Rivers. You've come to scout out the territory for your firm."

"Roland Cartier," I said in a French accent, getting to my feet.

"Good luck, Nick," Hawk said. "In the meantime we're going to keep a close watch on the people from the list, as well as the church headquarters in Chicago and their offices in New York."

Downstairs in Operations Readiness I was given a crash course in diamond types and identification, as well as the clothing and identification (including a battered French passport) of Roland Cartier.

My hair was cut in the European style, I was given shoes with lifts to bring my height up nearly two inches, padding to add forty pounds to my actual weight, and a strong dye which changed my complexion to that of a swarthy French Algerian of about fifty. Thick glasses and a Paris designer suit completed the transformation.

"Monsieur Cartier," the operations chief said, stepping away from the floor length mirror.

I bowed slightly from the waist, clicked my heels, and then went to the mirror. The change was startling. I didn't think even Pat would recognize me. Certainly no one from the church would.

"Your only problem is going to be the heat. It's summer there now, and damned hot. Because of the padding, you won't be able to go around in short sleeved shirts without a jacket."

"I'll manage," I said.

I remained at AXE headquarters that night, and in the morning took a cab out to the airport for my flight down to Miami with connections to South America.

Manaus (or Manáos as the Brazilians called it) was one thousand miles inland from the sea and was actually on the Negro River, which joined with the Amazon twelve miles downstream.

With a population pushing two hundred thousand, the city was the capital of the Amazonas Province and a port for ships of fairly high tonnage that steamed all the way upriver from the ocean to pick up rain forest products—mostly rubber.

It was big, dirty, bustling, and only two hundred miles south of the equator, and therefore unbelievably hot.

I wanted to stick around the airport to ask if anyone had seen Pat, Atterbury and the other two men show up here, but it would have been too much of a risk that someone from the church would find out that questions were being asked.

Instead, once I had cleared customs, I took a cab into the city where I checked into a nice hotel downtown.

I was given a room on the third floor, and from my balcony I was able to look out over the city to the docks and warehouses along the river.

The church had no interests in Columbia. It's holding was here in Brazil, so it was a safe bet that Pat and the others had already come this way and were heading upriver by now.

Somewhere up the Amazon the Reverend Franklin Knox held court. Coari was at least two hundred miles upriver from here, and there was no telling how much farther the church's installation was. Or even where it was. But wherever, Pat and Atterbury were there, or would be very soon.

I ordered up several bottles of cold beer and a light supper from room service, and while I was waiting for it, I stripped and took a long, cool shower.

Just as I was pulling on my robe, the waiter came with my order. I paid him, then went out on the balcony where I sat down to catch what little breeze there was.

The beer was ice cold and very good. I sipped it slowly as I ate the sliced cold chicken and boiled potatoes that had been sprinkled with vinegar and salt and pepper.

There was no airport at Coari; the town was too small for it. So Pat and others had to have left from here either by road or by river. I suspected they were traveling on the river. The roads back into the jungle would not be good.

A third possibility, however, was that the church maintained its own runway at its camp. If that was the case, they could have flown out of here.

But I didn't want to go back out to the airport. I didn't want to attract any attention. When I showed up at the camp, I wanted my presence to come as a complete surprise.

When I was finished eating, I went back into my room, retrieved my weapons from the luggage, then got dressed in a lightweight summer suit. Donning the glasses, I left my room, went down to the lobby, and stepped out into the humid tropical night.

From my room I could see the direction to the waterfront, and I headed that way now on foot. I took my time as if I was nothing more than a tourist out for an evening's stroll.

The streets were busy with traffic, and the closer I got to the river, the poorer the buildings became, and the rougher the people standing around appeared.

Within a couple of blocks from the river itself, I could smell a number of rich odors, among them mud, rotting wood, diesel oil from the ships, and raw sewage.

Poor people were everywhere; garbage lay rotting in the streets, and on almost every street corner prostitutes leaned up against the buildings scanning the passers-by for possible marks.

About a half a block up from the river, I entered a bar that obviously catered to seamen. Just inside the door I stopped a moment, and half the people ın the crowded room turned to look at me. None of them were smiling.

At the bar, the burly barkeeper came down to me, and I ordered a cognac plain in passable Portuguese with a slight French accent.

"On my mother's grave, the wog wants a cognac. Plain," the barman bellowed.

Several of his customers laughed.

I smiled and adjusted my thick glasses, then pulled out a hundred Cruzeiro note and slapped it down. "Cognac, plain," I said loudly, this time strengthening my French accent.

The barman, who was a full head taller than me, scooped up the note, stuffed it in his pocket, and then glancing at his friends, laughed, "You are in the wrong place, Frenchman. Now you'd better leave before you have an accident."

I adjusted my glasses again, pulled out another hundred Cruzeiro note and laid it on the bar. "Cognac. Plain!" I snapped.

The barman reached for the bill, but I grabbed his hand, pinning it to the bar.

An instant hush fell over the room.

"With two hundred Cruzeiros, every man in this bar should have a drink," I said.

The barman tried to struggle out of my grasp, but I was stronger, and I began to bend his hand backwards, putting a great deal of pressure on his wrist. With my left hand I adjusted my glasses again and smiled.

"It would be a shame if your wrist broke," I said.

"Carlos," the barman shouted.

There was a sudden movement behind me. Keeping my grip on the barman's hand, I stepped aside as an eighteen-inch-long billy club intended for my head, crashed down on the bar.

I kicked out with my right foot, catching the large, dark man in the groin, and as he started to double over, I brought my knee up, catching him full in the face.

He went down like a felled ox, blood spurting from a broken nose, and I turned back to the bartender, grabbed a handful of his shirt front with my left hand, and dragged him half over the bar.

"A cognac, plain!" I barked. "And set everyone else up with a drink. Including yourself."

I let go of the bartender, shoving him backwards, then pulled out my Luger and slammed it down on the bar.

"I came in here for a drink, and to find a *man* with a boat who is willing to make some money. A lot of money," I rattled in perfect Portuguese. "I did not come for a fight, although if I am made mad enough by you motherless whores, a fight is what you will get."

The bartender, rubbing his wrist, quickly poured me a large cognac and then set out a bottle of cheap rum for the others.

I reached down and grabbed Carlos, pulling him roughly up to the bar where I had to hold on to him lest he fall. "Someone take care of this one," I said.

Two men scurried up, grabbed the man, and hustled him around the bar into a back room.

I drank my cognac down, and the bartender poured me another. It was almost as if I was in some kind of a western movie, but these people were serious about it. What I had done was the only way to earn their respect.

"You mention a boat, Senhor," the barman said finally.

I nodded. "I wish to go up the Amazon."

"For what purpose . . ." the barman asked, but I slammed my fist on the bar.

"Ten thousand for the proper boat and crew," I said. "No questions asked."

I had everyone's attention.

"I only meant to ask what kind of a boat would you need? A speed boat, fast and powerful? A cargo vessel? A tug?"

"A boat capable of traveling with speed and comfort to Coari and beyond, returning with a cargo. A small but very valuable cargo."

"And the nature of your cargo, Senhor?"

"Enough," I said. "No more questions." I turned around to face the others who were staring at me. "There may be some danger. But if we find what surely we will find, I will double the amount of money agreed upon."

"To Coari?" one of the seamen asked.

"And probably beyond."

He shook his head and slumped back in his seat. The others did the same.

"Are you all motherless whores? Are you all women?"

"You were right, Senhor, when you said there would be danger," the bartender said from behind me.

I turned to him.

"There have been government troops in and out of that region for the past six months or longer."

"Why?"

"The Indians up there have been going crazy. There have been deaths, always preceded by lights in the sky." He shook his head sadly. "It is not a place to be. Coari, perhaps, but not beyond on the river."

It was possible the church was up there, I thought. They might have stirred things up just to make sure they were not disturbed by their neighbors.

"Then I will have to keep searching," I said, turning once again to the others, "until I find a man."

The comment stung, but for several seconds no one made a move. I grabbed my second cognac, drank it down, then slammed the glass on the bar and started to walk out.

An older man with white hair and a huge stomach got to his feet and shook his head.

"Do you want to leave this night, or will you wait until morning?"

"You have a boat?"

He nodded.

"Then you will make her ready while I return to my hotel for my things. We will leave within the hour."

The other man turned to the bartender. "Luis," he said. "If word of this leaves this despicable establishment, I will return and slit your ugly throat from ear to ear."

The bartender nodded solemnly.

"This way, Senhor," the fat man said. "I will show you my vessel first, and we will have a drink and talk. I will send someone for your things."

I grabbed my Luger, holstered it, then threw down two more hundred Cruzeiro notes. "A drink on me. And if word does leak out and this gentleman doesn't return to slit your throat, I will."

NINE

The fat man's name was Pedro Arimá, and his boat, the *Romāno,* was a forty-foot, shallow draft river tug that was probably old and battered twenty years ago. Now, looking at it, I had to wonder what kept it afloat.

"A humble boat, Senhor, but one that will surely do the job," Arimá said as we stepped off the dock onto the deck.

It was quiet here. Warehouses lined the broad wooden quay, and dozens of boats of every size, shape and purpose were either tied up, or anchored out in midstream. There didn't seem to be any activity.

"Where is your crew?" I asked.

"Tomorrow is Sunday, of course, and they have the day off. Only my cabin boy, Domingo, is here. I will send him for your things."

He turned to go below, but I stopped him. When he turned back his eyes were wide.

"I offer you no harm, Captain Arimá, if you do exactly as I have hired you to do. But if you play any games with me, it will go very hard."

He nodded slowly.

"The others back there were afraid of the river

above Coari. But not you. Why?"

"Oh, I am afraid, Senhor. Make no mistake of that. It is just that this ancient vessel is in need of repair. I am more afraid of losing her than I am of whatever will occur on the river."

"Good enough," I said. "When we are finished, I promise you there will be sufficient money to repair your boat."

Arimá smiled and nodded. "I will fetch Domingo now to bring your things. When he returns we will leave."

I followed the man below, where he rousted a young boy of ten or twelve. I gave him the name of my hotel and room number and enough money to pay my bill, and he hurried off the boat.

In the captain's pigsty of a cabin, Arimá poured us both cheap rum in dirty glasses, and when we both had taken a drink, he looked at me over the rim of his glass.

"What then, are we searching for above Coari?"

"We will know when we get there," I said.

For a moment the man let it ride. "You mentioned a cargo?"

"Yes," I said. "But nothing that will strain the capabilities of this vessel."

"What I mean to ask, Senhor, is shall I call my crew back? Will we need their muscle?"

I shook my head. "They won't be necessary. For now I merely want to get to Coari, where I will have to ask a few questions. After that I will tell you more."

"Coari is a very difficult town," Arimá said hesitantly. "There may be trouble if you are not careful."

"Trouble that you need not become involved

in," I said. "How familiar are you with the river above there?"

"I've been up it once, years ago, with my father."

"But not since then?"

He shook his head. "It is not a pleasant area. There are Indians there—who do not like outsiders."

"Then we will have to be careful," I said.

Domingo was back twenty minutes later with my bags, and within five minutes we had slipped our lines, and the aging diesel engine was pushing us slowly downriver.

I sat up on deck cleaning my Luger and smoking a cigarette, while Arimá was on the bridge above me.

Away from Manaus, and the city lights, the jungle closed in around us, although the river was very wide here.

It was about twelve miles down the Negro River before we came to its confluence with the Amazon, and swinging wide, well around the sand bars, Arimá took us out into the middle of the Amazon, and we started upriver.

There were a few ocean-going vessels anchored out here, in the much larger river, for the first couple of miles, but later we left them behind, and once again were alone.

The evening was hot and very humid. After I had cleaned my gun and finished another cigarette, I went below to my cabin and changed into some lighter clothing, removing the padding I was wearing as well as the thick glasses.

Apparently I had managed to get into Brazil and

up the river without alerting the church or the authorities. Once I started asking questions up in Coari, my disguise would no longer matter anyway.

Back up on deck, I climbed up into the wheelhouse. When I came in, Arimá glanced at me, then did a double take.

"When this is all over," I said softly, "you will forget that you have ever seen me."

"What are we after, Senhor, drugs?" he said. "If that is so, I will turn around right now. I do not want that kind of trouble."

"Not drugs," I said. "And nothing illegal."

"Then why the disguise," the man said fearfully.

"I will explain it later. For now your job is simply to get us to Coari."

Arimá was obviously troubled, but he had no more questions for me. "We will be in Coari by daybreak," he said. "Perhaps you should get some rest."

"You'll manage all right up here alone?"

He nodded. "Underway on the river, I never sleep."

"I am a very light sleeper," I said evenly. "And I would not take kindly to any kind of disturbance."

"You will not be disturbed, Senhor," Arimá said. "You have my assurances."

I nodded, then went back down belowdecks to one of the cabins, where I wedged my stiletto in the door before I lay down.

With my right hand on my Luger, with the safety catch off and a shell in the chamber, I fell asleep to the sounds of the laboring diesel engine and the water slapping against the bow.

What seemed like minutes later, I awoke to the sound of someone banging on my door. Sun streamed through the small porthole over my bunk.

"Senhor . . . Senhor, we are coming into Coari," Domingo was shouting.

"I'm up," I said in Portuguese, as I crawled out of the bunk and holstered my Luger.

I slipped my stiletto out of the door, sheathed it, and then opened the door. The young cabin boy stood in the corridor, a steaming cup of coffee in his right hand. He held it out to me, and I took it.

"The captain, he say you come up to the bridge now. He must talk with you before we dock."

"Right," I said. I took a sip of the strong, black coffee, then left my room, went up on the deck, and climbed up to the wheelhouse.

Arimá, his eyes puffy and red rimmed, stood at the wheel as he piloted the boat across the river toward a collection of rough wooden docks, beyond which was a small, dirty looking town.

"Coari?" I asked.

Arimá seemed very worried. "We will tie up at the public docks. But first I must know if there will be trouble here."

There was a great deal of activity on the docks. Large, flat-bottomed river boats were being loaded with wood, rubber and other things. Nothing seemed out of the ordinary. Nothing seemed threatening.

"Stay aboard and get some rest," I said. "I'm going into the town to ask a couple of questions."

Arimá looked at me. "Please, now tell me what we have come for."

"There is an American settlement someplace upriver from here. It is a religious settlement. A friend of mine is there. I want to bring my friend back."

"Many North Americans are in Brazil, Senhor. They run many of our rubber plantations. But a religious settlement? I have not heard of such a thing."

"It is here somewhere near. I will find out just where, and we will go there."

"There will be trouble," Arimá said. "I can feel it in my bones. There will be trouble."

"Even more trouble for you if you are not here when I come back. Do you understand?"

He nodded. "I will not leave you here, Senhor. Of that you can be sure. But I do not want trouble to fall on my head."

Domingo was down on the deck. And as we approached the public docks, I went down on deck with him, and the two of us leaped up onto the dock as we came in and tied the fore and aft lines to the thick wooden bollards.

Arimá cut the engine and joined us on the dock.

Our arrival elicited absolutely no attention from anyone on the busy dock. Workers, many of them Indians, scurried back and forth pushing hand-trucks loaded with bales and boxes.

"Is there no dockmaster here?" I asked.

"He will be around in his own sweet time," Arimá said. He reached out and touched my arm. "Coari is not like Manaus," he said. "The people here do not like gringos. They want to be left alone."

"I only have questions," I said. "For which I *will* get answers."

Arimá nodded. "And then we will go up the river."

"Yes."

"As I said before, there are Indians up there," he said, waving his hand in the general direction upstream. "Some of them are so deeply back into the forests, that they have seldom if ever seen a white man."

"What are you trying to tell me?"

"There are murderers up there. Cannibals. Even our own government soldiers do not go back too far."

"There are other river towns farther up," I said.

"Yes," Arimá agreed. "Very small, and very much more dangerous and isolated than even Coari. For us to go up the river, we will have to be very careful."

"We will go only as far as necessary, and stay only so long as it takes me to pick up my friend."

Arimá nodded. "We will wait here then for you. Be careful."

"Thanks," I said, and I walked down the dock and strode past the warehouses and riverfront offices, and then headed up into the town itself.

Coari was a town of about five thousand people. And if Manaus had been poor and dirty, this town seemed to be on the verge of starvation, with filthy people everywhere.

Yet there was money here. Beyond the town, in the low hills, there were some crops; and beyond that, in the forests, there were great rubber plantations.

Two blocks up from the docks was a village square. The police station was on the far side, a military Jeep parked out front with a soldier leaning against it.

On the opposite side was a large Catholic

church, and as I stood in the center of the square by a fountain and the public well, the church doors opened and freshly scrubbed peasants began filing out.

Some of the people headed away from the square up side streets, while others came across to the various shops and stores that were just now beginning to open.

A very old man, wearing a priest's garb, had stepped out on the front steps of the church and was saying goodbye to his parishioners as they left.

I waited until everyone had left the church, then started across.

The priest was turning to go back inside when he spotted me coming across the square, and he waited.

"Good morning, Father," I said mounting the steps.

"Good morning, my son," the priest said. "You wish to speak with me?"

"Yes. Could we go inside?"

The priest looked beyond me, and I turned in time to see two men in civilian suits coming out of the police station. They got into the Jeep, the soldiers jumping in the front seat, and then they were gone up a side street.

"Of course," the old priest said, and he turned on his heel and entered the church.

I followed him up the aisle, where at the altar he genuflected as he crossed himself, and then led me to a small office to one side.

We sat down across a small table from each other in the dark, cool room. A young Indian girl came in a moment later with glasses and a bottle of wine.

"You will drink with me?" the priest said. "Perhaps you will have breakfast as well?"

"If it is not too much of a burden, Father," I said. The church was obviously very poor.

He smiled and said something in a strange language to the Indian girl, and she giggled and left.

I took a few hundred Cruzeiros from my pocket and laid them down on the table. The priest looked at the money and then started to object, but I held him off.

"I am not paying for my wine and my meal, Father," I said. "I do not mean to insult you that way. But you give your people comfort; allow me to help."

The priest smiled, then nodded. "As you wish, Senhor," he said.

A minute or two later, the young Indian girl was back with two bowls and wooden spoons, a pot of thin soup, some bread, and several bananas that had been sliced, fried in butter and then sprinkled with brown sugar.

When she was gone, the priest poured us both a glass of the deep red wine, and ladled out some of the soup.

"You are a North American. Perhaps Boston?" the priest asked as we ate. The food was rough, but very good.

"Washington, D.C.," I said.

"Ah . . . your nation's capital city," he said. "You are many miles from your home, Senhor."

"I come seeking a friend."

The priest seemed amused. "A friend, you say. You have no friends at home?"

"It's not like that, Father. My friend has come down here. Against her will, I fear."

"Kidnapped?" There was something in the old man's eyes.

I nodded. "By the Church of the Final Reward. They have a camp near here. . . ." I let it trail off. The priest had gone white, and his hand trembled so badly he spilled some of his wine.

He put his glass down and got up. "You will have to leave now," he said.

I got up. "All I want to know, Father, is where their camp is located."

The priest was shaking his head. "You will leave now."

"I know it's somewhere upriver from here. But you must tell me where. Exactly where. I need your help."

"I cannot help you, Senhor. It is bad. Very bad here for us."

"Then I will have to ask elsewhere. Someone here in this town will be able to tell me," I said. I turned and started to leave the room.

"Wait," the priest cried.

I turned back. "I am afraid for my friend and others like her."

"I am afraid for my people as well," the priest said. "If I tell you where . . . will you leave Coari immediately this morning?"

"Yes," I said. "And no one will ever know where I got my information."

The priest waved that off. "By now, everyone in this village knows that you are here and have spoken with me. When you leave upriver, they all will know what you have learned here."

"If it would be better for me to obtain the information elsewhere . . ."

He shook his head and motioned me back to the

table. We both sat down, and he poured more wine.

There was a small window that faced the west, in the general direction of upriver. He glanced that way and shuddered.

"Five years ago when they began that abomination, we all thought it was a fine thing they were attempting to do," the priest began. He did not look at me. "It was to be a place, far away from worldly cares, troubles and temptations."

"A noble idea," I prompted after a silence.

The priest nodded sadly. "I thought as much. But then the stories began."

"Lights in the sky at night?"

The priest looked sharply at me. "You have heard some of the stories?"

"Only that, in Manaus," I said. "And that government troops had been sent up here."

"Yes, but only for a few days. It was the poor Indians in the back country. They were killing settlers and travelers on the river."

"Was that normal?"

"Not for the last hundred years. But within a few months of the cult establishing its camp up there, the Indians became frightened of the devil lights, as they called them, and began hearing voices and seeing visions, telling them to kill or be killed."

It was neat. The Indians kept everyone away from the church's facility.

"The government sent troops up here, but they left without doing a thing."

"Why did they leave so suddenly?" I asked.

The priest looked at me. "I do not know, Senhor. I only know that this town, and everything above, all the way to Tefé, is not safe."

"Where is the camp?" I asked leaning forward.

"It is thirty miles from here. Up the Arauá River, which flows into the Amazon not far away."

"The Arauá," I repeated. "Are there guards there? Is the place like a military installation?"

The priest was shaking his head. "I do not know, Senhor. I personally have never been there, nor will I ever. But they would have no need of guards, in any event."

"Why?"

"The Indians control all that territory. No one from Coari goes up the river nowadays."

I nodded, drank some of the wine, and then got to my feet. "Thank you, Father, for your help."

"Will you then listen to one piece of advice, my son?"

"Yes."

"Return to Manaus this morning. Leave here and forget your friend."

I shook my head. "Too much has happened for me to do that, Father. But thank you for your concern."

"Then may God go with you, my son," the priest said. He turned and left the room by a back door, leaving me alone.

I stood there for a long moment before I turned, went back through the church, and stepped out the front door.

There were a great many people on the square now. Many of the shopkeepers had set up tables and booths outside, making the entire area seem like a bazaar on a holiday.

No one was paying me the slightest attention, but as I came down the steps and started across the square, I got a funny feeling that I was being watched, and that everyone here knew exactly what was going to happen.

Across from me, the army Jeep was parked once again in front of the police station. The two soldiers stood there, smoking, watching the crowd.

A half a dozen brown-skinned Indians, razor-sharp machetes stuck in their waist sashes, were squatted down near the fountain, and as I passed they looked up at me.

For an instant it seemed as if everyone on the square held his or her breath, when suddenly the Indians leaped to their feet, the machetes raised over their heads, and they came after me.

I managed to sidestep the first one, slamming my left foot into his shins, and he went down, but then the others were nearly on top of me, and there was no room for me to maneuver.

I took off in a dead run, threading my way through the crowd, upsetting display tables and booths as I ran, while behind me, the Indians screaming wildly, took up the chase.

Circling around the square, I passed the soldiers in front of the police station, and they were laughing as they pointed at something happening on the opposite side of the square.

A few seconds later I had ducked down the side street that ran behind the warehouses on the dock. As I continued to run, I pulled out my Luger.

I came around the last warehouse a minute later, and the dock which had been busy earlier, was now deserted, except for Arimá's boat, which was tied up.

He and the boy, Domingo, were on the deck looking out toward the river.

"Start the engine!" I shouted, fifty yards away.

They turned around, and for an instant they just stared at me.

"The engine!" I shouted again.

Then Arimá was scrambling up the ladder to the wheelhouse as Domingo grabbed up a fireaxe and hacked through the bow line.

I made it to the boat, and jumped aboard as the engine came to life, and Domingo began hacking at the stern line with the big fireaxe.

I spun around as the first of the Indians reached us. One of them threw his machete, just missing me, the long blade sticking into the side of the boat.

Snapping off four quick shots, three of the Indians went down. The fourth leaped off the dock, slamming into me as we pulled away, the diesels roaring.

We went down in a heap, my Luger jerking out of my grasp, and for a few wild seconds I was fighting for my life, the big Indian swinging his machete wildly around my head.

Then I managed to flip him to the side, and as he raised the machete overhead, I snapped a right hook to his jaw. His head snapped back, and he dropped the machete. I scrambled up, grabbed his body, and heaved it over the side into the river.

A dozen townspeople had joined the Indians on the dock, and they all were shouting at us, but we were too far out into the river now for them to do anything. It didn't seem as if any of them wanted to give chase. They had tried to stop us, without success, and now they were going to let us continue upriver—very possibly to our deaths.

TEN

The people still lined the public dock as Arimá took us well out into the river, and then he began to swing us in a big arc, bringing us with the current so that we were heading downriver.

Domingo had come back to where I stood, and wide-eyed, he began swabbing the blood off the deck.

I tried to motion for Arimá to turn us back upstream, but he refused to look down at me. Quickly I scrambled up the ladder to the wheelhouse, but he had locked the door and would not look at me.

Pulling out my Luger, I stepped back, and holding on to the handhold, I fired one shot down at the latch.

Arimá jumped away from the wheel as I slammed the door open and stepped inside.

"Upriver, Captain," I shouted.

"No, no, Senhor, please. We will all be killed!"

"Then get off the boat here," I snapped, stuffing the Luger back in its holster. I grabbed the wheel and spun it hard to starboard, the boat sluggishly responding.

Two small powerboats had pulled away from the public docks and were starting across to us. By the time I had our boat headed back upstream, they had come within a couple of hundred yards.

Arimá saw them the same time I did, and he came across to the wheel.

"I'll take it," he snapped. "There is a rifle behind us in the locker!"

"Upriver," I said.

"Si . . . Si," Arimá said, angling away from the two boats.

On the back wall of the wheelhouse was a large, wooden cabinet, the open padlock dangling from the hasp. I yanked it open. Inside was a twelve-gauge scatter gun and a very old Winchester 30-30. There were a couple of boxes of shells in the bottom of the cabinet.

I grabbed the double barrel shotgun and the box of shells and hurried out of the wheelhouse, down to the deck.

Domingo was standing at the rail staring at the rapidly approaching boats. Each contained half a dozen armed men.

"Go below!" I shouted.

Domingo looked at me with fearful eyes.

"Below!" I shouted, and the boy finally started to move. "And stay there no matter what happens," I said.

I cracked the shotgun open, shoved two shells into the barrels and snapped it shut.

The boats were less than fifty yards away when I brought the shotgun up. One of them swerved aft, so I leveled the barrels at the other boat and fired, spraying the entire boat with buckshot.

Quickly I reloaded the shotgun, but the boat had swung around and was heading back to shore. I raced around to the port side of the wheelhouse just as the second boat was coming up to us.

When they saw me, three of the men started to raise their rifles. Shooting from the hip, I fired both barrels at less than ten yards.

Two of the men were knocked backwards out of the boat; the third was driven backwards over one of the seats, and the boat peeled off, accelerating aft.

I watched them go, the two men in the water sinking out of sight, a wide trail of red mingling with the current.

They had meant to kill us, and I had acted in self defense. But there would be no Brazilian court of law that would agree with that. I was a foreigner, and I had killed several Brazilian citizens, including four Indians on the docks.

Getting up to the church's encampment was turning out to be no picnic. But getting out of Brazil was going to be even tougher.

Around the other side of the wheelhouse Domingo was standing in the doorway that led below, a wide grin on his face.

The two boats were pulling up at the docks far behind us now as we continued upriver.

"You take plenty good care of those sonsabitches all right," the young boy said in English.

I stared open-mouthed at him for a long moment, and then had to laugh out loud.

"Domingo!" Arimá shouted from the open door of the wheelhouse above.

"Si?" the boy said, stepping out on the deck and looking up.

"Make us coffee and breakfast, you little bastard," Arimá shouted.

"Si," the boy said happily. He winked at me, then turned and disappeared below.

I went back up to the wheelhouse where I put the shotgun and shells away. "I don't think they'll bother us anymore."

"Did you find out what you wanted to know?" Arimá asked.

I joined him at the helm. About a mile ahead the river branched left and right. "Yes," I said. "The church's camp is about thirty miles away, up one of the branch streams."

Arimá looked at me. His complexion was wan.

"The Arauá," I said and he nodded.

"It's the left channel. Very bad."

"Why is that particular channel very bad?"

"It is not merely that one, Senhor. It is all of the back channels. There is no one up them except for the Indians." He shook his head. "Very bad. Very bad. I will not go there."

"Yes you will," I said. "It will be daylight when we go in there, and still daylight when we come out."

"Are you so sure you will be able to convince your friend to return with us?"

I grabbed his arm just above his elbow. "What do you know about the church?"

"Nothing, nothing, I swear it."

I looked into his eyes. He was frightened, but I didn't think he was lying. I let go of his arm and looked at my watch. It was a few minutes after nine A.M. We would probably make it up to the church's camp around noon, if the old priest's directions were correct and Captain Arimá didn't do anything foolish.

After everything that had happened in Chicago

and Washington, and now in Coari, there was no
doubt that the church was expecting me to show up
at their camp. But they also were aware, I was reasonably certain, that I did not work for Amalgamated Press, and that I was a man not easily dis-
couraged.

I sat up on one of the tall pilot stools in front of
the forward windows as Arimá guided the boat
into the mile wide left channel, his knuckles white
where he gripped the wheel.

Whatever the church was expecting from me
now, I didn't think they expected me to show up on
their doorstep in the middle of the day, demanding
an interview with the Reverend Franklin Knox
himself. But that's exactly what I was going to do.

With any luck, my appearance with Arimá and
the boy would throw them off momentarily—at
least long enough for me to see Pat, then get her
aboard the boat and get out of there.

After that would come the difficult part: getting
out of Brazil in one piece. I was sure there would be
a reception committee waiting for us near Coari.

"There are three channels leading back from this
one," Arimá said breaking into my thoughts.
"The Coari to the south, the Urucu in the middle,
and the Arauá to the north."

"We go north."

The river was still very wide here, but in the distance I could see where it narrowed dramatically,
swamp lands near the northern shores giving way
in the distance to forests.

"Is there no other way, Senhor?"

"No," I said.

A few minutes later Domingo came up to the
wheelhouse with a pot of coffee and a couple of

mugs. He set the things down, went below, and when he came back, he brought with him our breakfast of eggs, small strips of beef and a flat, tasty bread.

He took the wheel, and as Arimá and I ate, he guided the boat toward the outfall of the Arauá, still miles to the north, as the sun continued to rise in the equatorial sky.

The Arauá was a narrow channel, barely a hundred yards wide at most spots. But it was deep. Domingo stood on the bow deck taking soundings with a lead line, and calling up the depths to Arimá, who guided the boat with one hand while he hung out an open window.

I had cleaned and reloaded my Luger, loaded the 30-30 and the scattergun, and I sat now on the samson post just forward of the wheelhouse.

"That's wrong," Arimá shouted down. Domingo turned around to look up at him.

"It is the reading, Captain," the boy said.

"Get up here and take the wheel."

Domingo shrugged, laid the lead line down, and climbed up to the wheelhouse. A moment later Arimá came down, grabbed the lead line and heaved the sinker overboard.

The channel here was at least fifteen feet deep.

"What is it?" I asked.

Arimá turned to look at me, then glanced back upstream. "I didn't think we would get this far," he said. "This stream should not be this deep. Maybe five or six feet, not fifteen."

I got up and joined him at the bow. "Could you be mistaken?"

He shook his head. "No, Senhor, I am not mistaken." Again he looked upriver. "This stream has been dredged. It's been deepened to take large boats."

"The church," I said half to myself.

"Must be a very rich, very powerful church," Arimá said. "A church that is doing some kind of a business up here that requires a deep water access."

"How far yet?" I asked.

He shrugged. "We have come twenty-five miles now. So if you were correct, and the church camp was thirty miles from Coari, then we are close."

He coiled up the lead line, and as he was bending over to drop it into a deck box, an arrow passed over his head.

"Down!" I shouted. I dove aft, below the level of the scuppers, a dozen arrows silently passing overhead, two of them smacking into the side of the pilot house with low twangs.

I grabbed the 30-30 and slid it up the deck to where Arimá was lying on his belly, then grabbed the scattergun.

Domingo had ducked down below the level of the windows, and every now and then he peeked up over the sill in order to steer the boat.

Another volley of arrows came in, this time several of them crashing through the windows of the wheelhouse, and the others smacking into the hull of the boat.

As fast as the attack had begun, however, it stopped. Except for the sound of the diesel engine, there was silence.

I chanced a quick peek over the rail, but there was nothing in sight other than the jungle that closely lined both banks.

Arimá still lay on his stomach, one hand clutching the rifle, his face buried in his other.

As I sat up, I looked up at the wheelhouse. Domingo stood there grinning.

"Did you see anything?" I called up to him.

"Nothing, Senhor," he said from the open window.

Arimá rolled over. He was shaking. "We will turn around now and go back."

"No," I said, getting to my feet and scanning the river banks on both sides. I had a fair idea why the attack had come, but I couldn't understand why they had given it up so fast.

"We go back now!" Arimá roared, getting to his feet. "This is my boat, and I say where she goes."

Ignoring him for the moment, I went aft and looked downriver from where we had come. There was nothing back there except the silent jungle. Nothing. Why had they stopped so suddenly?

When I turned and went forward, Arimá was climbing up to the wheelhouse, the 30-30 still clutched in his left hand.

"If you try to turn back, I will shoot you," I said evenly.

Arimá stopped and looked at me. I held the shotgun loosely under my right arm, and I could see that he was trying to judge whether or not I really would carry out my threat.

His fear of the Indians won out.

"We will both do what we must," he said, and he took the next step up.

"Goddammit," I swore, reaching out for the ladder when an arrow smacked into Arimá's left shoulder.

He cried out in pain, lost his footing on the ladder and half fell and half stumbled down on top of me, both of us hitting the deck.

I scrambled out from under him, popped up over the rail, and fired both barrels of the scattergun into the forest, then ducked back down.

Arimá was screaming and crying in pain and rage where he lay. The arrow had gone almost completely through his shoulder, missing the bones. He had to be in extreme pain, but he was in no immediate danger of dying.

"Listen to me," I said to him. "You're going to be all right. We'll get you some help."

"Poison," he cried, his eyes wild, spittle drooling from his open mouth. "The arrows are poison."

"Senhor! Senhor!" Domingo called from the wheelhouse.

I looked up. He was gesturing to something upriver. Quickly I scrambled forward to where I had left the shotgun shells on the deck near the samson post, reloaded the gun, and popped up over the rail, ready to fire. But I suddenly stopped, my breath catching in my throat.

We had come around a gentle curve in the stream that suddenly opened to a huge lagoon that had to be several thousand yards across.

On the far shore was a long, modern steel and cement quay, several powerful looking boats tied up there, and at least a hundred people all wearing long flowing white robes lining the dock.

Inland, a huge area had been cleared from the jungle, and in place of the trees and dense undergrowth, a small, but very modern town had been constructed.

There was a wide mall leading up from the

docks, and from where I knelt looking over the rail, I could see well tended flower beds and carefully planted trees and fountains up the middle of the mall, with numerous stores and shops on both sides.

An ultra modern church of glass and steel, in the form of a highly stylized pyramid, dominated the far end of the small town from a small rise. Behind it was some sort of a wide field ringed by bleachers.

The effect of the buildings, of the dock and of the people, many of them waving now as Domingo headed the boat their way, was stunning.

The place was beautiful.

I stood up as Domingo throttled down, the boat easing the last twenty yards.

Several men, also clad in the white robes, were coming down the mall toward the dock in a dead run. One of them was carrying a black doctor's bag.

Arimá was still crying and cursing where he lay, and this close in now, many of the people waiting on the dock could hear him, and they appeared to be deeply concerned. Almost fearful.

Domingo closed in on the dock, expertly throwing the boat in reverse at the proper moment, so that we just nudged the soft timber fenders.

Several men from the dock scrambled aboard, one of them stepping respectfully past me, and tossed lines over to where others tied us up.

As the diesel engine died, the men who had come down from the mall came aboard, and the one with the doctor's bag immediately tended to Arimá, giving him a shot of something before he ordered two of his assistants to carry the captain off the boat.

"Be careful with him, Brothers," the doctor said.

Gently they lifted Arimá off the deck and carefully carried him across the dock and up the mall.

The doctor closed his bag and came forward to where I still stood, the shotgun cradled under my right arm.

He stuck out his hand. "I'm Doctor Bernard Wilcox, originally from Buffalo, New York."

I shook his hand. A silence had descended over the gathering as everyone watched us.

"I think you already know who I am," I said evenly.

The doctor smiled. "Indeed, Mr. Carter," he said. "You've caused us no end of trouble, you know, but Brother Knox is a forgiving man."

"Is that why he's tried to kill me?"

A sigh rippled through the crowd.

"No one has tried to murder you, Mr. Carter."

"And the fire?"

A dark expression crossed the doctor's face. "The two . . . renegades who did that have been excommunicated. In fact, Brother Knox wants to personally apologize for that unfortunate incident. We were so happy and relieved when we learned that neither you nor Miss Staley were seriously injured."

"Is she here now?"

The doctor smiled again. He seemed almost like an animated cartoon character, and he was starting to get on my nerves.

"Indeed. She came last night. She's anxious to see you as well. When she heard you were coming, she was beside herself with excitement."

"Fine," I said. "As soon as you have patched up Captain Arimá, please send her down here, and we will leave you alone."

"Heavens no. Brother Knox would skin me alive if I didn't insist on extending the hospitality of Reward."

"Reward?"

He chuckled. "That is the name of our village here in the forest. Hostile on the outside, but a genuine 'Reward' once you arrive."

"A half hour," I said.

The doctor stepped forward and reached for my arm, but I backed up and raised the shotgun, pointing it at his midsection.

"I'm in no mood for your silly bullshit, Doctor," I snapped. "I want Miss Staley down here within a half an hour."

The doctor almost seemed to be on the verge of tears. "Oh dear," he said. He looked over toward the others on the dock. "One of you good people go fetch Sister Staley. Tell her Mr. Carter has arrived and would like to speak with her."

When he turned back to me, he shook his head.

"Now, off this boat," I snapped. "We'll be leaving shortly. Have your people bring Captain Arimá back as well."

Domingo stepped halfway out of the wheelhouse door. "Senhor," he called down to me.

I glanced up at him. "Get the boat ready to leave."

The boy shook his head. "We do not have the fuel to return, Senhor," he said.

"We can give you fuel," the doctor interjected.

"Now!" I snapped.

The doctor turned to the people on the dock. "Would someone be so kind as to refuel this vessel."

Two men broke away, crossed the dock and entered one of the buildings.

"I'm sorry that you cannot find it in your heart to remain, at least for a day or two. Brother Knox had planned a dinner tonight and tomorrow will be a festival of the Lights For Departing Souls."

"Nick!" someone shouted my name.

I looked up as Pat, wearing one of the white robes, came bounding down the mall toward us. She seemed excited, and . . . happy.

The crowd on the dock parted to let her pass, and I was stepping past the doctor to help her aboard, when something sharp and very hot pricked my neck just below my left ear.

Almost instantly a roaring began to fill my ears, and I could hear Pat shouting my name.

I spun around on my heel, bringing the shotgun to bear on the doctor. But he reached out, grabbed the barrel, and easily twisted the gun out of my hands.

Staggering back I grabbed for my Luger, but I couldn't seem to make my fingers work, and the doctor's smiling face seemed to expand overhead, while Pat kept calling my name and laughing.

ELEVEN

I awoke rested and relaxed minutes or hours later. I was lying nude on my stomach on a padded table of some sort, while soft, but strong hands massaged the muscles in my shoulders.

For a minute or two I just lay there, my head turned to one side. From what I could see, I was in a large, airy room. Windows high up on the wall let in the afternoon Brazilian sun. And somewhere behind me I could hear water splashing and smell the rich odors of plants.

"I'm so happy you are awake finally, Mr. Carter," a woman said behind me.

I turned my head and looked up. My masseuse was a beautiful young woman with long, red hair and freckles all over her body. She was nude, the nipples on her small breasts hard, and her lips slightly parted as she smiled at me.

"How long have I been here?" I asked thickly. Whatever drug I had been shot with made it difficult to speak. It was as if I was still half asleep.

"Several hours," the girl said. "Can you roll over now? I'll do your front."

The girl helped me roll over on the table, and she began working immediately on my shoulders, and then on the muscles of my chest.

"What is this place?" I asked after a minute or two.

"The Palace of Pleasure," she said. "And my name is Charlene."

Knox had quite a setup down here. His own personal kingdom, with all the comforts, and more, of home. "The man and boy I came with. Where are they?"

"Oh, they're just fine, Mr. Carter. Little Domingo is playing with the other children, and Captain Arimá is resting at the Clinic."

"Where is Pat Staley?"

"Sister Staley is getting ready for our dinner tonight," Charlene said gaily. "It will be a lovely dinner. And afterwards there will be the festival of lights. It'll be wonderful, you'll see."

I was beginning to come fully awake, my head finally clearing. And I looked closely at the young woman. Her eyes were wide and dilated. She was on drugs. There was no doubt about it. Probably everyone down here was.

"I want to see her," I said.

"See her?" Charlene asked. "Who?"

"Pat Staley. I want her to come here now."

Charlene giggled. "Oh no, she does not work here in the Palace of Pleasure. There are only a few of us in the guild."

I sat up on the table, brushing her hands away. The room spun a moment as the girl stared openmouthed at me.

"I'm not finished yet, Mr. Carter," she said. "Please . . . please lie down and let me finish."

"We're done," I said. I got down off the table,

and she had to help me for a moment as the room
spun again.

"You're not ready yet," she said.

"Where are my clothes?"

"There are fresh robes for you when we are finished—"

"My clothing, Goddammit!" I shouted. I
grabbed her arm and pulled her to me. "Where are
my things?"

She was shaking her head. "I don't know. You
were brought here to me, like . . . this."

I shoved her aside and went across the room to
a low, wide bed set amidst a riot of green plants
that grew in some places as high as the tall, slanted
ceiling. A white robe and sandals were laid out for
me, and I quickly put them on.

"Oh please . . . please Mr. Carter, you can't
leave here," Charlene was crying.

Ignoring her, I went across the room, down a
wide, plant-filled corridor and out the front door.

The building I had been in was huge, a broad
porch running its length. Several men and women
lay asleep on lounges, while white-robed attendants massaged their temples or fanned them.

Charlene had pulled on a robe and she came out
behind me. "Please come back, Mr. Carter.
Brother Knox will be so displeased if you won't
accept our hospitality."

"Where is the Clinic?" I said.

"Why do you want to go there?"

"I want to speak with Captain Arimá."

"If I take you there, will you come back with
me?"

I looked at the girl. "After I see the captain, I
want to speak with Pat Staley. And then I may

come back here with you."

A couple of the other attendants had looked up, and they started toward us.

Charlene waved them back. "It is all right, Sisters," she said. She took my arm and guided me down off the porch and across the mall, the huge church behind us to the right, the river and docks below to the left.

Music was playing from somewhere, and there were several people out and around on the mall, some of them wandering past the many fountains, others seated at pleasant-looking sidewalk cafés.

We crossed the mall and went up to a large, white building without windows that was just below the church.

"Captain Arimá is here," Charlene said.

We mounted the steps and entered the building. Just inside the front door was a very large room with a desk and several medical equipment cabinets at the far end. To the right were four machines used to air-inject drugs into patients' arms. They were lined up in four columns, and I suddenly understood just how Knox and his henchmen kept the people down here so docile. Probably on a daily basis, every man, woman and child was marched in here and given a dose of some kind of a tranquilizer.

We went across the room to the left and went through a set of double doors down a wide corridor that opened onto a small, four bed dispensary.

An old man lay in one of the beds, and Arimá lay in another, his shoulder bandaged. He was asleep.

"There is the captain," Charlene said. "Now can we go?"

"Just a minute," I said. I went across to Arimá and gently shook him awake.

He blinked several times until he finally focused on my face. "Senhor," he said thickly.

"How do you feel?" I asked, keeping my voice low. There were no medical staff in here at the moment, but Charlene stood by the door watching me.

"Fine . . . fine," Arimá said. "Are we leaving now?"

"Soon," I said. "Do you think you can travel?"

"Sure . . . sure, tomorrow perhaps. Or maybe next week." He smiled vacantly. They had him on the drug, whatever it was.

"I'm coming back for you," I whispered. "Tonight."

"Mr. Carter, can we go now please?" Charlene asked from the doorway.

Arimá's eyes closed, and he smiled as I straightened up and went back to Charlene.

"I want to see Pat Staley now," I said. "And then I will go back with you."

"I can't take you to her. You will have to go back to the Palace of Pleasure, and I will bring her to you."

"All right," I said. "And I'll want my watch and my clothes and my other things brought to me."

"I will try, Mr. Carter," the girl said.

We went down the corridor, across the large room and back outside. It seemed to be about four or five in the afternoon, and it was very hot. As we walked across the mall, back to the Palace of Pleasure, I looked down toward the docks. I could see Arimá's boat still tied up where we had left it, and I just caught a glimpse of a flash of white in the wheelhouse, but then it was gone.

There was someone aboard the boat. The Reverend Knox was not going to let us out of here without a fight. And I was not going to leave without Arimá and the boy, as well as Pat.

Back in the Palace of Pleasure, Charlene and I went back to my room. "Promise that you will remain here, and I will get Sister Staley."

"And my things," I said.

She nodded and then turned and left. As soon as she had disappeared around the corner, I hurried to the tall, padded table and shoved it over next to the wall just below one of the tall windows that faced the mall.

I climbed up on the table and was just barely able to see outside. I watched as Charlene emerged from the building and went across the mall, then cut down toward the river.

She entered a long, low building.

"I'm glad to see that you are feeling better, Mr. Carter," a man said behind me.

I spun around. Michael Seidelman, wearing a white robe, sandals on his feet, stood grinning in the doorway.

"Sister Anderson will be back in a minute or two with Sister Staley," he said. "Why don't you come down from there."

I jumped down from the table as Seidelman came across to me. He held out his hand, but I ignored it.

"A slick setup you have down here," I said.

"Why did you come here?"

"For Pat Staley," I snapped. "And I *will* take her back with me."

"For the moment you are in no position to do much of anything, Mr. Carter."

"I could kill you here and now with my bare hands," I said in a low voice.

Seidelman laughed, but it had a false ring. "And then what? Your boat captain is in no shape to be of much help. The boy is happy here . . . it's paradise to him. And you'll be very much surprised when you speak with Sister Staley."

"You've given her the tranquilizer," I said.

Something flashed in Seidelman's eyes, but he shook his head. "We've given her nothing but the facts of life."

"And Atterbury?"

"Him too, although he did help convince Sister Staley of the truth."

I was dressed in nothing more than a robe and sandals; I had no weapons, and I was still suffering slightly from the after effects of the drug I had been shot with. There wasn't much I could do. At least not at the moment.

"You understand that I work for the Amalgamated Press and Wire Services, and that my people know exactly where I am."

"I understand that you *may* work for the news service, although I have my doubts," Seidelman said. "But I do not have any doubts that if anything happened to you here, there would be others after you. So, nothing will happen to you, Mr. Carter. At least not here."

Charlene came to the doorway with Pat Staley.

They stopped a moment when they saw Seidelman was here.

"Nick?" Pat said.

"I want to be alone with her," I said to Seidelman.

He looked at his watch. "It's five-fifteen now. At six-thirty sharp Charlene will return and you and Miss Staley will join us for dinner. Brother Knox is most anxious to speak with you."

"And afterwards?"

"That will depend upon you, Mr. Carter. If after speaking with Brother Knox you still want to leave us, you will be escorted by boat back up to the Amazon, just above Coari. From there you will be on your own."

Seidelman turned, went across the room where he took Charlene's arm, and they left.

Pat was smiling, her face radiant. Like the others, she was dressed in a white robe, sandals on her feet. Her hair had been done up in the back, and she wore a small gold medallion on a headband.

She came slowly across the room to me, and I took her in my arms and held her close for a long time.

When she looked up, we kissed deeply, her body pressed against mine.

"I missed you, Nick," she said when we parted. "I wanted to leave you a message, but I was told it would be for the best if we parted cleanly."

"How are you, Pat?" I asked.

She smiled again. "Just fine now that you're here, Nick." She looked over at the wide bed, then up again into my eyes. "We have time now. Let's make love."

"I'm taking you back with me tonight," I said.

She took my hand and led me across the room to the wide bed.

"Do you understand what I'm saying to you, Pat? We're leaving tonight."

"All right," she said offhandedly. Her eyes seemed too bright, but her behavior too lethargic. It didn't seem as if she was on any drug at the moment, and yet she wasn't herself.

She stepped back and pulled off her robe. She was nude underneath, her body firm and lovely. She stepped out of her sandals, then lay down on the bed.

"Come to me, Nick. Now. Please. I need you."

I took off my robe and sandals and joined her on the bed. Languidly she snuggled closer to me, her legs entwined with mine as she caressed my chest and nibbled on my ear.

"This room is bugged, Nick," she said so softly I could barely hear her words.

I drew her even closer and kissed her neck. "Are you all right?"

"They had me on the drug," she whispered. "I was busy with the banquet preparations today, and I managed to get out of taking mine at noon."

She moaned, rolled over on her back, and pulled me atop her. When I entered her, she moaned again, burying her face in my neck.

"Atterbury is in on it. They drugged me at his house and then brought me down here. I've signed a will leaving everything to the church."

We were making love then, and her last words were slurred as she began to respond in earnest. For the moment, then, we lost ourselves in each other, forgetting where we were and the trouble we were in.

When we were finished, we showered together in a small stall, and then slipped into a large hot tub set across the room from the bed.

She came to me in the tub, and we clung to each other as if in a loving embrace, which was partly true. "Can you get us out of here?"

"Do you think you can find my clothing and my weapons?" I whispered.

"No," she said. "Some of Karsten's men—he's head of security along with Seidelman—have your things up at the church. No one can get near the place except those on church business."

"Are there any guards here with guns?"

"None that I've seen. But we've all been told not to wander away from the town, especially at night. The Indians here are cannibals."

I tried to think this out. Arimá's boat would be far too slow, and Domingo had said it was low on fuel anyway. That meant I was going to have to take one of the church's boats. There were a couple of them tied up at the docks that looked sleek and very fast.

Getting down there with Pat, Arimá and the boy, however, was not going to be easy. It was a certainty that Seidelman, Karsten, and their goons would be watching out for just that.

"What's going on tonight?" I asked.

"There's supposed to be a big banquet of some sort to celebrate the new arrivals . . . me included."

"Where?"

"I don't know. Up in the church, probably.

That's where everything of importance around here takes place."

"What about the field? I saw it on the way in. It looked like a sports stadium. What's it used for?"

"I don't know," she said. "But it has something to do with the festival of the Lights of the Departing Souls, which is also going to happen later tonight, and then something really big is supposed to happen tomorrow night. But no one does much talking about that, and I'm afraid if I ask too many questions, they'll realize I didn't take my tranquilizer."

"All right, Pat, we'll be getting out of here soon. Probably tonight. But try to avoid your drug tomorrow if we can't get out of here by then. And be ready at a moment's notice to run."

"I'm frightened, Nick," she said, holding on to me tightly. "And I keep thinking about Don."

"We'll get out of here, Pat. I promise you."

Charlene came back forty-five minutes later as Pat and I were drying off and dressing. She apologetically held out my watch, my cigarettes and my lighter.

"This was all I could get for you, Mr. Carter," she said.

I took them and strapped on my watch and lit myself a cigarette. "Thanks anyway for trying," I said.

Charlene turned to Pat. "You're to go back to the dormitory. Sister Therese is waiting for you there. We all have to get ready for the banquet." She seemed excited.

Pat nodded, lowering her eyes, but then she looked up at me, a dull, vacant expression on her face. "Are you sure, Nicholas, that you will not stay here with us in Reward?"

"I'll think about it," I said. "But I'd rather you return home with me."

Pat slowly shook her head. "This is my life now, my darling. I am one with the Final Reward." She turned and glided out of the room.

"Sister Staley is a lovely woman," Charlene said.

"So are you," I said gently.

The girl blushed. "I must return to the dormitory to make ready. Brother Michael will be by momentarily for you."

She turned and left the room.

I went back to the bed where I strapped on my sandals, and when I turned around, Seidelman was standing in the doorway. He was wearing a long white robe with gold trim at the neck and hem and a gold sash around his middle.

His right hand was in a deep pocket. He pulled out my Luger slowly and pointed it at me. "An ugly, but deadly weapon I am told," he said.

"It's given me good service."

"I merely wanted you to know that I am armed, and I will not hesitate to use it if I find the necessity arises. In addition, my people will be closely watching you throughout the banquet. The slightest wrong move on your part will result in your immediate death. Do I make myself perfectly clear?"

"Will I get to meet Brother Knox?" I asked.

"Of course. You will be seated right next to him."

"Aren't you afraid I might attack him?"

Seidelman laughed out loud. "Not in the slightest," he said.

TWELVE

Seidelman followed me out of the Palace of Pleasure and directed me up the hill toward the ultra modern church building. Many people were walking slowly up the mall toward the huge doors at the front of the building, some of them in small groups, some of them in long, almost military lines, but none of them singly.

It was noticeably cooler now, and the sun was low on the western horizon. It got dark fairly early on or near the equator, which was just as well, I thought. Whatever was going to happen, would probably happen tonight. Darkness would give us needed cover.

Near the top of the hill I was able to spot a number of security men with their hands in their pockets. They circled the crowd and flanked the doorway. All of them were watching me.

As we passed, they nodded at Seidelman still behind me, and then we were up on the broad, marble step that led to the entrance.

The church was at least two hundred feet on a side and probably a hundred and fifty feet tall at the peak. Just inside the main doors, the crowd was moving through a broad hallway, down a wide corridor, and into the main chamber at the center of the pyramid.

As Seidelman and I emerged from the corridor, I stopped in my tracks, my breath catching in my throat.

The vast hall was magnificent. A latticework of steel beams and sharply angled sheets of plate glass and mirrors rose in a complex array from about thirty feet above the floor all the way up to the peak. Long, curved banquet tables set with crisp linen tablecloths and silver service, formed huge arched tiers, all facing toward a raised dais at the center, upon which was set a single long table that slowly rotated.

At the far end of the hall, a twenty-piece orchestra was playing what sounded like Debussy, the music barely competing with the hum of a thousand voices in the packed church.

"It's wonderful, isn't it," Seidelman said at my elbow.

I glanced at him. "With money you can do almost anything," I said.

"If you'd only stick around for a day or two, you'd see just how true that is."

"No thanks," I said.

"A pity," Seidelman replied, and we moved off across the hall toward the raised dais. "You'll be seated directly next to Brother Knox, on his left side. I'll be right next to you, the Luger under the table."

We were stopped repeatedly by people who wanted to say hello to Seidelman, and by others who were frankly curious about me.

At one point I thought I had spotted Pat seated

with a number of other women, but when I looked again, I couldn't see her.

Seidelman escorted me up on the dais, and to a seat at the table. The center chair, the one Knox would be sitting in, was tall, gracefully curved and made of transparent plastic or glass. It didn't match anything else in the hall and seemed oddly out of place.

I sat down, Seidelman taking his place next to me, and immediately a young woman appeared at the front of the table and poured us both champagne.

Seidelman's associate, Larry Karsten, came up on the dais, nodded at us, and took his seat a couple of chairs down from the center. A moment later, Pat, escorted by two women, came down one of the aisles and stepped up on the dais.

I started to get up, but Seidelman stopped me.

"Another half inch off your chair and there wouldn't be a thing I could do to save you," he said.

"Hello, Nicholas," Pat said. She sat down in the chair just to the right of Knox's. Champagne was poured for her, and she picked up the glass and sipped, ignoring me.

She was doing the right thing. If any of them got wind of the fact that she had not taken her tranquilizer, they'd force her to take it.

But seeing her here, seated next to Knox's position, gave me the shivers. I knew exactly what was planned for her.

Gradually the last of the people filed into the hall, took their places, and a silence began to descend, broken only by the lovely strains of the music.

Looking out across the crowd, I could see that everyone seemed expectant, as if they were waiting for something spectacular to happen. Even Seidelman had the same look on his face, as he hunched slightly forward in his seat.

I was about to ask him about it, when the orchestra broke off its playing, sounded a drum roll, and every light in the vast hall went out, plunging us into total darkness.

Immediately I felt the barrel of the Luger jammed into my side. "Do not move a muscle, Carter," Seidelman's voice came from the dark.

An eerie, high-pitched keening sound began from somewhere directly overhead, rising slowly in pitch and volume so that the sound seemed to fill the entire hall.

About the moment it became unbearable it suddenly ceased, and a blindingly bright blue light came on, illuminating the Reverend Franklin Knox seated regally on his modernistic chair.

A sigh rippled through the crowd, and as they began to applaud, lights came on directly over each table, including ours.

The applause swelled to a thunder, and people began cheering and screaming and whistling. I couldn't help but stare at Knox. There was something wrong with his image. At first I thought it was my eyes, or the harsh blue light that caused his figure to waver.

Pat was staring at him as well, and suddenly I realized what was wrong, and why Seidelman had not been concerned with the fact I would be seated so close to him. Knox was not here. What we all were looking at was a holographic projection of his image.

I glanced up toward the area just above him. There was a strong blue light. Behind him there was another light, and from the floor a third light shown through the chair.

Knox was somewhere else seated at a table that matched this one. Totally protected.

His image turned toward me, and he smiled, the gesture totally devoid of humor or warmth. His eyes seemed to glow with a deep red light, and his skin was cast in a pale blue pallor.

"Welcome to Reward," he said, his voice booming powerfully across the hall.

Instantly the thunderous applause ceased, plunging the vast hall into absolute silence.

"Thank you for your hospitality, Brother Knox," I said evenly.

Knox laughed, the sound booming. "This, my brother in sin, is merely a way station on the long, arduous road to the final reward." He turned to look out over his audience that was hanging on his every word. "Tonight we will dedicate this banquet to all the lost souls of this world who have yet to see the light. To all the avarice and mendacity, to all the pestilence and famine, to all the wars and money mongers, who can be saved if only they would reach out their hand for salvation." He reached out his hands, as if he was beseeching his congregation. "Will you be saved?" he cried.

"Yes!" the crowd roared.

"Will you be saved?" Knox screamed louder.

"Yes . . . oh yes, Brother Knox, we will be saved!" the audience screamed.

"Then join me in our feast. Join me in the festival of the lights tonight. Join me in a day of fasting on the morrow. And join me, Brothers and Sisters, for the celebration of the Final Reward!"

At least three dozen white-robed waiters and waitresses seemed to appear out of nowhere, and began serving food and more wine to the throng.

Two young women served our table, neither of them approaching Knox, who sat there looking over his congregation.

It was a great show, I had to admit. And I suspected that no one down on the main floor could tell that Knox wasn't really there, that his image was nothing more than a technological trick of electronics.

From time to time Knox sipped at a glass of wine, but he never looked right or left. He kept staring out across the hall as the dais continued to slowly rotate.

Twice I managed to catch Pat's eye, but each time she just nodded at me vacantly, then went back to her meal.

The orchestra had started up again, and there was a low hum of conversation and occasional laughter. I just picked at my food which consisted of oysters on the half shell, an excellent French onion soup, a fresh spinach salad, pheasant and wild rice, but I drank a second glass of the good wine, and then sat back with a cigarette.

About two hours after the banquet had begun, the orchestra again stopped playing, and a drum roll sounded. A silence fell, and the same eerie high-pitched sound began. The lights went out, leaving Knox's figure starkly illuminated. He waved.

"Let the festival of the lights begin in one hour," his voice boomed, and then he was gone, the hall completely dark until the house lights came up slowly to more applause.

Seidelman pushed back his chair and got up as the people down on the main floor began leaving.

I got to my feet. "I'd like to speak with Pat for a moment," I said.

Seidelman nodded, and I turned and went around Knox's chair to where Pat was still seated. Karsten had gotten up. He glared at me and then moved off as I bent down to kiss Pat's neck.

"I know where you're staying. I'll try to come for you late tonight."

She looked up at me and giggled, a vacant expression in her dilated eyes. They had gotten to her. They had discovered she had not taken her tranquilizer.

"What did you say, Nicholas?" she asked.

Christ. "I said, it was a lovely dinner."

"I'm so glad you enjoyed it," she said.

I shook my head and sighed deeply as I straightened up. It would have been difficult getting her out of here with her cooperation. Now the task was going to be next to impossible.

Seidelman was waiting for me at the edge of the dais, and I went over to him.

"What's on the agenda now?" I asked.

"Brother Knox would like to speak with you, in person, in his quarters before the festival of lights begins."

"An exclusive interview?"

"Something like that," he said. He stepped down from the dais, and I followed him to the back of the hall, several of his henchmen coming right behind us.

We went through a wide door, down a plushly-carpeted, softly-lit corridor, and then into an elevator that went up rapidly, emerging from the sloping side of the pyramid and through the floor of a large projection from the building.

The doors opened on the most opulent suite of rooms I had ever seen in my life. I had been to Paris and Monte Carlo, to Berlin and Rome, and to Buenos Aires and Mexico City, but never had I ever seen anything to match Knox's living quarters.

Gold icons, fine paintings, soft leather furniture and what appeared to be a carpet sewn of mink and ermine filled the apartment, whose back wall was clear glass from floor to ceiling, looking over the sports stadium and the jungle beyond.

Knox himself, a brandy snifter in hand, stood with his back to us, looking out the windows. People were already filling the stadium, and he was nodding as he watched them.

He was a very tall man, nearly seven feet, with a husky build and a thick shock of black hair.

"Be so kind as to pour Mr. Carter a drink, Brother Michael, and then leave us," Knox said.

Seidelman complied, returning to me with a brandy snifter of what tasted like a fine cognac, and then he and the guards stepped back onto the elevator and were gone.

"Is it really you?" I asked. "Or another clever projection."

Knox turned toward me. "You have caused me no end of trouble, Mr. Carter. Or would you prefer to be addressed by your alpha-numeric designation . . . N3, I believe it is."

I was momentarily stunned. There were damn few people in the world who had that information, outside of AXE.

"Killmaster status, I believe," Knox was saying. "Curious."

Then I understood where he had gotten the information. From Pat. And suddenly a deep, very dark anger began to well up inside of me. They had her on tranquilizers. But what other drugs had they used on her to obtain that information? What had they done to her mind?

"You would like very much to kill me at this moment, but it would be of no avail, even if you could accomplish it."

I took another sip of the cognac. The drink could have been drugged, or poisoned, but I didn't think Knox had called me up here to kill me that way. There was something else. Something deep in his eyes, almost a sadness, that made me think differently.

"I don't understand," I said, looking around the apartment.

"No, you don't. Your kind never have. Nor will you ever. Because understanding of this comes from the heart, not the head."

"Bullshit," I said sharply. "You have a great racket going here. Last I heard, you and your church were worth more than a billion dollars."

"Seven-point-eight billion U.S. dollars, at current market prices," Knox said.

"Which makes you the richest man in the world."

"Yes," he said flatly. He turned his back on me again and looked out the window at the rapidly-filling stadium. "What have you come looking for, Mr. Carter?"

"I came for Pat Staley," I said.

"I'm afraid that's not possible," Knox said. "Although I knew it would be impossible, I had almost hoped that once you arrived, you could somehow be convinced that what we are doing is right and good."

"Convinced? With some fancy parlor tricks?"

"Have you seen an unhappy person since you've been here?"

"If there was enough Valium to go around, the entire world would be happy, Knox. Which means nothing."

Knox shuddered. "Get out of here, Carter. Take the elevator downstairs, and you will be escorted back to the despicable little boat that brought you. Arimá and the boy are already aboard."

"Not without Pat."

Knox spun around, and I tensed thinking he was going to spring at me.

"Get out of here. Leave us in peace, or I will take you where all of us are going tomorrow night!" he screamed like a wild man, spittle flying from his lips, his teeth bared.

"You're crazy," I said. "What in God's name are you planning for tomorrow night?"

"The Final Reward," he screeched. "Stay and you will be a part of it. Leave and your life will be your own!"

The elevator doors opened behind me. "Let's go, Carter, your boat is waiting."

I turned to face Seidelman and two of his guards. They all had guns pointing at me.

What was going to happen wasn't scheduled until tomorrow night, which gave me at least twenty-four hours. Not enough time to bring in help, but certainly enough time for me to come up with something.

I drank the rest of my cognac, set the glass down on one of the low tables, and without looking back at Knox, stepped aboard the elevator, and rode down with Seidelman and the other two.

They escorted me back through the church, out the front door, and down the mall toward the docks. The town seemed deserted. Everyone by now would be up at the stadium.

"About my clothing and weapons?" I asked, as we walked.

"Your clothing is aboard the boat, which we have refueled and reprovisioned for you. But you will go unarmed in peace."

"To be massacred by the Indians."

"Whatever fate decrees, so be it," Seidelman said with satisfaction.

The diesel on Arimá's boat was idling when we came down to the docks. I stopped by the boat and turned around to look up beyond Seidelman and the others, toward the church. Behind it, the night sky was lit with a soft glow from the lights around the stadium.

"Tomorrow night will be another Jonestown, with one important difference," I said, looking back at Seidelman.

The man had a half-smile on his lips, but he said nothing.

"You and Karsten and your goons won't be taking the fall, although Knox will." I shook my head. "He's quite crazy, you know. I think he actually believes in all this mumbo jumbo."

"Get aboard, Carter."

"What about Pat?"

Again Seidelman smiled. "She'll be well taken care of."

I almost sprung at him then, but I held myself back. Pat wasn't the only one at risk down here. Suddenly the stakes had risen much higher. Suddenly there were more than a thousand potential and likely victims of Knox's madness and Seidelman's greed.

"I will be seeing you again, Seidelman," I said.

"I don't think so," he replied.

I turned and jumped aboard the boat. The little boy, Domingo, was up in the wheelhouse, and he waved down at me when I looked up.

I released the dock line at the bow, then went back to the stern and released that line. Immediately Domingo eased us away from the dock, and we headed across the lagoon and downriver.

As I started up the ladder to the wheelhouse, I looked back in time to see Seidelman and his two guards heading away from the dock, while one of the large, sleek speedboats pulled away and fell in behind us.

They were going to make sure that we didn't turn around and attempt to come back. Either that, or they were going to follow us until we got well away from the town, and then attempt to sink us.

I hurried the rest of the way up to the wheelhouse and went inside.

Domingo looked frightened, but he was doing well with the boat. Arimá was not here.

"Where is the captain?" I asked, joining him at the helm.

Domingo looked up at me, his wide brown eyes filling with tears. "He is dead," he choked out the words. "They say it was the poison that kill my papa."

"Your *father* . . ." I said half to myself in English, but the boy understood.

He nodded his head. "He was my papa. They brought him below. The sonsabitches!"

He was crying hard now, and I took the wheel from him with one hand, while I cradled him against me with the other.

"Why?" he cried. "Why?" Over and over. I had no answer for him.

We made it across the wide lagoon in a couple of minutes, and then plunged down the deep, but narrow Arauá, the night closing in around us now that we were away from the town.

The speedboat was a hundred yards behind us, its running lights clearly visible in an inky backdrop.

"You must listen to me now, Domingo," I said.

The boy pulled away and looked up at me. He nodded, sniffling.

"I want you to search the boat for weapons. Guns, ammunition, knives, machetes—anything we can use."

I glanced back. The other boat was still there about a hundred yards aft.

Domingo had started for the door.

"Is there any fuel aboard other than diesel for the engines?"

He nodded. "Paraffin."

Kerosene. It would work. "Good," I said. "After you have searched for weapons, bring the paraffin out onto the after deck."

Again he nodded, and then he scrambled out the door and down the ladder.

If they meant to sink us, they would be in for a very large surprise.

I was reaching up and flipping off the cabin lights, when I noticed the softly illuminated fuel gauges. One of them was on empty; the other needle hovered just above the empty mark. They had not refueled us! It had never been their intention to let us go. It still didn't answer the question, however, of their exact intentions, although I thought it was likely that they wanted us to run out of fuel here, without weapons. Easy pickings for the Indians who had attacked us on the way up.

Keeping the boat steadily on course, I kept glancing back. The speedboat remained a hundred yards behind us. Probably waiting for us to run out of fuel.

Domingo returned a few minutes later carrying a ten-foot-length of chain, and a machete.

"Was that all?"

Domingo nodded. "Si. The paraffin is on the after deck as you wished. There are two cans, maybe eight liters."

"All right. Take the wheel. Give me two minutes to get below and get ready, then turn off all our running lights and throttle back. But listen up for my order to get the hell out of here at full throttle."

Domingo looked up at me, a grin starting. "We're going to kill the sonsabitches?"

"We're going to try, kid. We're going to try."

THIRTEEN

Outside on the after deck of the boat, near the stern, I opened one of the deck lockers, and with the machete cut a ten inch section of thick rope from a coil, then quickly frayed one end of it.

The speedboat was still behind us, its running lights bright points in the night.

Opening one of the four-liter cans of kerosene, I dipped the frayed end of the rope into the fuel, soaking it well. Then I pulled out my lighter and waited for Domingo to flip off the lights and throttle back.

The speedboat following us was made of fiberglass, the hull fairly thin and light for speed; whereas this boat was constructed of heavy wooden timbers with a thick hull and a bow strong enough to bring down a barn.

Our chances of success were slim, but I could think of no other way.

Our running lights were suddenly flicked out, plunging us into darkness. An instant later Domingo throttled back, the wake we had thrown catching up with us, slopping us forward until we settled down in the water.

Quickly I picked up the open can of kerosene and poured it into the water, holding it well out away from the stern.

The speedboat behind us suddenly revved up, and I could see by her lights she was riding high up on the water.

Once I had emptied the can of kerosene into the river, I looked up over my shoulder. Domingo was hanging out one of the wheelhouse windows.

"Full throttle!" I shouted.

He ducked back inside. At the same moment I flicked my lighter and set fire to the frayed rope soaked with kerosene. It flared brightly in the night, and Domingo jammed the throttle full forward and we shot ahead.

I flipped the burning rope overboard, and the kerosene lying on the surface of the water ignited in a small patch that worked its way rapidly into a large sheet of flame that rose twenty feet above the river.

Working my way admidships, I scrambled up the river into the wheelhouse and took the helm from Domingo.

Behind us the river was a sheet of flame, beyond which the speed boat was invisible. But even as I watched, the flames were beginning to die down.

I angled the boat over toward the left bank, and when I figured we had come as close as we could get, I slammed the helm hard over to the right. The boat responded sluggishly even though we were running at full throttle, and for a couple of anxious seconds, I didn't think we'd make the turn without running aground. But then we were heading upstream, directly toward the dying flames.

Domingo was standing braced next to me, a wild look on his face. For him, this was all nothing more than a simple matter of vengeance. They had killed his father. He wanted to kill them.

"Hang on," I shouted over the roar of the engine.

About twenty yards from the now nearly dead fire, I spotted the big speedboat riding at a slight angle in mid-stream, and I braced myself for the collision.

Something crashed through one of the wheelhouse windows at the same moment I spotted a flash from the forward deck of the other boat.

They were shooting at us. "Down!" I shouted, and Domingo dropped below the level of the windows as several more shots were fired.

The speedboat was starting to move, trying to get out of our way. But instead of turning his bow toward us, to present a much smaller target, the helmsman was turning downstream, laying his entire flank open.

At the last moment, I could see white-robed men leaping off the deck of the boat into the river, and then I ducked down below the level of the windows, and we crashed. Our boat seemed to lift up into the air, a deep-throated, grating sound reverberating through the night, and then we canted to the right and settled at the bow.

I jumped back up and threw our boat into reverse. We had struck the speedboat just below its bridge, shoving it over on its side.

As we backed off, finally pulling free, I could see water pouring through a huge hole in the hull. The speedboat rapidly settled, bow first, her stern riding high up, but then sinking rapidly out of sight.

"Turn the lights back on," I shouted, turning the wheel over to Domingo, and then heading out the door, down the ladder to the deck.

Several men were screaming wildly around the wreckage. At first I couldn't tell what was happening until our lights came on.

The river was boiling and blood red. Three men to one side of the oil slick, where the speedboat had gone down, were screaming and thrashing in the water that seemed to have come alive with fish.

Piranha. The river seemed alive with them. And there wasn't a thing I could do for the poor devils in the water.

Domingo held the boat against the current, and within a few seconds the water was quiet again. The only sign that anything had happened here was a slight oil slick and a few pieces of floating debris.

Domingo had seen what happened, and I could see him up in the wheelhouse with a large, feral grin on his face.

We circled the area for several minutes looking for survivors, but there was no one, and I finally climbed back up to the wheelhouse, took the helm from Domingo, and headed back upstream toward Reward.

"We going back to kill the rest of them, Senhor?" the boy asked. He was excited. His eyes were wide.

"We're going back to save the other people. No more killing."

"They killed my papa!" Domingo shouted.

"There's been enough killing," I said again. "No more." But even as I said it, I knew it wasn't likely that that would happen. There was going to be more fighting. A lot more, before this was over.

The fuel gauge needle was right on the empty mark as I angled the boat over to the right bank, throttling back so that we were barely crawling against the current.

I figured we were about a mile downstream from the town, but if we ran out of gas here, we would drift farther away. There would be no swimming to shore, and I didn't believe we had enough fuel to get us all the way to the docks. We were going to have to go ashore here.

"Go below, and as soon as we hit the bank, jump ashore and make us fast to a tree," I told Domingo.

He left the wheelhouse, scrambled down to the deck, and hurried to the bow line as I gently eased the boat over.

The moment we touched, he jumped over the side with the bow line. A minute later he scrambled aboard, hurried aft, grabbed the stern line and jumped ashore again.

I shut the engine down and flipped off all the lights. Grabbing the chain and machete Domingo had found, I went down to the deck as he was coming back aboard. The boat was secured.

With the boat lying still in the water, it was very quiet here, and nearly pitch black. Finding the town would be easy. We'd just have to follow the river upstream for about a mile, and we'd run into the docks.

I wasn't worried about that. It was the Indians. Their attack on us out in the river had been understandable. Yet the fact that they had backed off so easily was almost as bothersome as the fact that I had seen no defensive measures in the town.

It was almost as if the church and the Indians had some kind of an agreement, some kind of a pact together. The Indians apparently never attacked the town. But what did Knox and the others give them in return? What held the Indians off?

I left the chain on deck; it wouldn't do us much good in the thick underbrush anyway. I stuffed the machete into my belt and jumped off the boat onto the shore, the ground wet and springy beneath my feet.

Domingo followed, and we struck out toward the town, the vague outlines of a plan beginning to form in my mind.

Within twenty yards, the jungle had become so dense and dark that we were not able to see the river, only the vague outlines of the thicker trees around us.

I had visions of stumbling around out here all night, becoming hopelessly lost. I was about to turn back toward the river, when a streak of light crossed the sky, and then was gone.

Domingo and I stopped in our tracks and looked up. Only snatches of the night sky were visible through the treetops, and for a few moments I wasn't completely sure I had seen anything. But then another thin beam of light crossed the night sky from the west.

"What is it?" Domingo asked in a small voice. He was beginning to get frightened.

A third and a fourth light beam flashed in the sky, and I suddenly knew what we were seeing. Everyone had talked about a "festival of lights" tonight at the stadium. It was starting now, offering us an easy way back to the town.

More light beams of many different colors crisscrossed the sky, and I set out directly toward it, Domingo right behind me.

Within a quarter of a mile, we emerged from the dense jungle, finding ourselves on the opposite shore of the lagoon.

Across from where we stood, we could see the docks. There was still one speedboat tired up down there, but as far as I could tell, there were no guards posted.

From this point we could see the town, which was mostly in darkness, the church lit in red, blue and green lights. Beyond was the stadium, from where the light beams were flashing across the sky.

"What are the lights, Senhor?" Domingo asked once more in a small voice.

They were laser beams, I could see that. But what their significance was, I had no idea. I didn't think Knox and the church did anything just for show; so there was probably some meaning to the light show. But what?

"I don't know," I said, looking down at the boy. "But I'm going to find out."

"I'm coming with you," Domingo said, stepping back.

"To the boat over there. We're going to take it, and you're going to stay aboard. As soon as I get Pat, we're getting out of here."

"You won't leave me?"

"I won't leave you. I promise."

We worked our way slowly around the lagoon, coming at length to the pilings that held up the end of the dock. We crouched there in the shadows.

Still no guards were visible. They were probably

all up at the stadium for the light show which was still going on. But I didn't want to take any chances with Domingo.

"Stay here," I whispered. "If I make it to the boat, you can follow. But if anything happens, get out of here."

The boy nodded. I pulled the machete out of my belt and climbed up on the dock. I stayed there a moment, and then keeping low, raced down the wide dock directly toward the speedboat.

As I passed the opening up to the mall, I looked up toward the church. The entire town seemed deserted, but from here I could hear the crowd up at the stadium cheering.

Quickly I scrambled aboard the boat, stopped a minute to listen, then climbed up the outside ladder to the bridge.

There was no one there, and within a couple of minutes I had looked through the entire boat, confirming that no one was aboard.

Domingo came silently aboard as I was prying open a cabinet in the forward cabin.

The lock parted with a loud snap, and I threw open the door. Inside were three M16 automatic rifles and loaded clips of ammunition stacked in the bottom.

I grabbed one of the rifles, loaded it, and then pocketed a couple of extra clips.

"No matter what happens, I want you to stay here on the boat," I said, closing the cabinet door and hanging the lock back on the hasp.

We went back out on the deck. "You can watch from here," I said. "If anyone comes down to the dock, hide yourself."

"You won't leave me," the boy said.

"No," I said looking into his eyes. "But if I'm not back by morning, I want you to take this boat and get the hell out of here. Get back to Manaus, if you can, and call the authorities."

The boy finally nodded and I jumped back down to the dock and headed quickly up behind the buildings that faced the mall, keeping low and in the shadows as much as possible.

When I reached the dispensary, the last building at the top of the mall before the church itself, I could see the stadium about two hundred yards away. The bleachers were filled with people, and the laser beams flashing up into the night sky came from equipment set up in the middle of the field.

The rear door of the dispensary was unlocked, and just inside I stopped a moment to listen. But there were absolutely no sounds other than the people cheering in the stadium.

I hurried through the dispensary, down a long corridor, and into the main room at the front where I went immediately to the three machines used to air-inject the tranquilizer.

Laying my rifle down, I pulled the machete out of my belt and started on the machines, damaging them as much as I could, while making as little noise as possible. I cut hoses and wires, pried parts loose, and smashed the various dials and controls.

The machinery would be fixable, given time. But I only wanted to delay tomorrow's scheduled injections at noon. If the entire congregation came off the tranquilizer, there would be at least some of them willing to fight.

I couldn't handle Knox and his crew alone. Nor did I want to simply run off and leave his congregation to whatever he had planned for them.

I slipped out the front door and stood a moment on the dispensary porch watching and listening for any sign of posted sentries. But as far as I could tell, there was no one anywhere on the mall, or even up by the church.

Checking first to make sure the safety was off and a round was in the chamber of my M16, I sprinted down off the porch and across the top of the mall to the wide steps leading up to the church entrance.

The doors were still open, and just inside I stopped to catch my breath and look back the way I had come. I half expected to see someone coming after me, but there was no one.

I turned and went down the corridor into the huge main hall. The tables had all been cleared from the banquet, the chairs all back in place, and the dais was standing stationary.

Only a couple of dim lights high up in the latticework were on, providing just enough light for me to make my way across the hall and into the back corridor to the elevator that led up to Knox's quarters.

Like the dock and the mall, this place was deserted too. My luck was running high at the moment. If it continued to hold just a little longer, it was just possible I'd pull this off.

I punched the button for the elevator, then stepped back, raising the M16 to my hip. The doors slid open, but no one was in the car, and I stepped inside.

The doors closed automatically and the elevator started up.

Knox was the center of the entire organization. If I could get to him, it was possible that I could not only gain Pat's release, but the release of everyone else down there. Just how the hell I'd get them all out was another question; but I would deal with that when the time came—if it came.

The elevator bumped to a halt, and I raised the M16 as the doors slid open.

Knox's apartment was in darkness, except for the light coming through the glass wall from the stadium far below.

I stepped off the elevator, the doors closing behind me, and quickly searched the apartment. Besides the living room, there was a spacious master bedroom with a large, round bed, a huge bathroom with a sunken tub and a sauna, a small kitchenette, and a dining nook. The place was empty. Knox was evidently either down on the field or in the control room with the holographic projector.

I made myself a sandwich in the kitchen, grabbed a cold bottle of beer from the refrigerator, and went back into the living room where I sat down on one of the thick chairs in front of the window.

The light show was still going full force, multicolored beams of light stabbing high into the night sky, almost like fireworks on a Fourth of July celebration.

Tonight was the festival of Lights fot the Departing Souls, as they all called it. Apparently a harmless ceremony leading up to a day of fasting tomorrow, and then something tomorrow night. The Final Reward, Knox had said, was coming tomorrow night. If he meant what I thought he did, it was going to have to be stopped.

I had just finished my sandwich, and had drunk the last of the beer, when I heard the elevator coming up.

Jumping up and grabbing the M16, I stepped away from the glass wall, moving into the deep shadows in the corner.

The elevator stopped, the doors slid open, and the Reverend Knox stepped into the living room, Pat Staley right behind him.

"Stand very still and I won't kill you," I said.

Knox and Pat both stopped in midstride as the elevator doors closed, and I stepped out from the corner.

"Nick?" Pat said vacantly.

"You!" Knox hissed stepping forward.

"Stop!" I shouted. Knox complied. "I won't hesitate to shoot you down," I said.

"What do you want?"

"The three of us are leaving here. You're going to provide an escort for us down to the docks. I have a boat waiting for me there."

"You'll never get out of this building.

I smiled. "You'll be the first to die if anything happens."

"You're crazy!" Knox screamed. "You're going to ruin everything!"

"You should have thought about that when you caused Pat's brother to kill himself," I snapped stepping forward. "And you should have thought about it even harder when you came after me."

"What are you doing, Nick?" Pat asked, holding her hands out to me.

"We're leaving this place, right now," I said. There was definitely something wrong with her. She was on the tranquilizer, but there was something else the matter with her. They had brainwashed her or something.

"No, Nicholas," she said. "Don't you see, Brother Knox is correct. It is beautiful here. And tomorrow night, at the Final Reward, everything will be perfect."

"Listen to her," Knox said.

"We're getting on the elevator," I said, coming a little closer to them. They both backed up a step. "Call the elevator, Pat."

She shook her head.

"Are you going to shoot her if she doesn't comply?" Knox asked. He was smiling now.

Pat was staring at me, her mouth open.

I raised the M16 a little higher, pointing it directly at Knox's chest. "Call the elevator, Pat, or I will kill Brother Knox."

"No!" Knox shouted, but Pat turned and hit the elevator button, the doors coming immediately open.

"All right, step aboard," I said.

"You'll never get out of here," Knox said, but he and Pat both backed into the elevator.

The doors started to close as I jumped aboard. I jammed the barrel of the gun into Knox's chest. "I want no trouble," I said softly.

We started down, Knox's eyes locked onto mine, Pat watching us, a horrified expression on her face.

At the ground floor the doors opened and we stepped out into the empty corridor and started across to the main hall.

"Why are you doing this to us, Nick?" Pat asked, walking ahead of me.

"I'll explain later," I said. "For now you've got to trust me."

We stepped through the doors into the main hall, and Pat stopped a moment. "No . . . Nick, no . . . don't do this."

"Don't you remember Don? Don't you remember how he jumped out the window?"

She was nodding, a smile on her face. At that moment I almost shot Knox for what he and his people had done to her.

"He's in a better place now, Nick. We can all be there together."

"Let's get down to the boat, and I'll explain it all there. Can you do that for me?" I asked reasonably.

She looked uncertainly from me to Knox, who nodded. We then started across the wide hall, Knox right behind her. I brought up the rear.

"You'll never get that far," Knox said to me over his shoulder.

"We'll see . . ." I started to say, when I heard what sounded like a crowd roaring outside, and Knox laughed.

FOURTEEN

There was a huge commotion in the corridor opposite where we stood, and we all stopped as hundreds of screaming, shouting people burst into the main hall.

"Arise my people, and cast out the infidel!" Knox screamed.

I raced forward to where he stood, his arms over his head, grabbed him around the neck, and hauled him back a couple of steps.

The crowd roared even louder, answered by another mass of people streaming in from the corridor we had just left.

Other people burst into the hall from doors on the left and right, all of them screaming and shouting.

"Stop or Knox dies!" I shouted, but my voice was lost in the din as the mass of people advanced on us from all four directions.

"Oh Nick . . . please," Pat cried, and although I could not hear her, I could pick out what she was saying.

Knox was hanging loosely in my grasp and was not struggling with me. I raised the M16 over my head and fired a short burst, the shells breaking the glass and mirrors overhead, some of them whining off the steel beams.

Still the crowd advanced, and I suspected that even if I began firing into them, they would not stop. They were all on drugs, and evidently all hyped up after the festival of lights at the stadium.

I shoved Knox away and turned and raced to the middle of the hall, where I jumped up on the dais. The crowd surged forward totally surrounding me, and for a few brief moments I was certain they would come up on the dais and tear me down. But then they stopped.

Knox came forward, his people making a respectful path for him, until he stood just below me, his hands outstretched.

"Escape is impossible, Brother," he said. "You can not kill all of my people."

Out at the fringes of the crowd I spotted Seidelman and several of his men. They had Domingo. One of Seidelman's goons was holding a gun to the boy's head.

"Give it up and come with us in peace, Brother," Knox was shouting to me. "We will offer you no harm, on my word. Tomorrow you will participate in the day of fast with all of us, and in the evening, the Final Reward will be yours."

I have been in difficult situations in my life. But this was the first time I felt truly overwhelmed. I was armed. Yet there was simply nothing I could do to get out of here. Killing Knox would do nothing but hasten my own death, without having the slightest effect on what I knew was going to happen tomorrow night.

Alive, however, there was a possibility I still might be able to get us all out of this.

I clicked the safety back on, laid the rifle down on the table behind me, and clasped my hands behind my head.

Knox beamed his approval. He jumped up on the dais with me, grabbed the gun, threw it out to one of Seidelman's men in the crowd, and then took my machete and handed it down as well.

"You may put your hands down, Brother Nicholas," Knox said gently. "We are all friends here."

I complied, and the crowd began to break up, turning and leaving the hall through the four doors.

Pat left with them, and within five minutes I was alone with Knox on the dais, four of Seidelman's men armed with pistols standing below.

Knox shook his head sadly, stepped down from the podium, looked up at me one last time, then turned and strode across the hall, back toward the elevator.

"Convert him," he shouted over his shoulder. "Make him mine!"

"Down off there," one of the guards said roughly when Knox was gone.

I jumped down off the dais, and immediately two of the guards grabbed my arms at the elbows and yanked them back, while a third stepped up and gave me an injection in my neck just below my right ear.

I flinched with the sharp prick and started to struggle out of their grasp, but my legs suddenly began to get wobbly, a roaring sounded in my head, and a sense of peace and well-being seemed to course through my body, like waves on a beach.

Within a few seconds the guards released my arms. One of them took my hand and helped me walk along, down the aisle, through the corridor and out the front doors.

The lights from the stadium were out, and most

of the people were heading back to their rooms when I crossed with my escorts to the Palace of Pleasure.

Charlene, my masseuse from earlier, was there on the porch waiting for us. She wore a broad smile. "Brother Nicholas, you don't know how much we worried about you here," she said.

She took my hand and led me inside, my guards leaving us. Everything around me seemed to be hazy as I went with Charlene into the same room where I had been brought before.

Gently she undressed me, helped me take a shower, and then when I was dried off, walked me back to the wide bed where she laid me down.

She was nude, and suddenly she was in the bed with me kissing me everywhere and caressing me, her lovely breasts brushing against my chest and then my legs, and I could feel myself responding. It was as if I was in a dream.

She straddled me, and I slipped inside her at the same moment she broke something under my nose, and a sharply sweet odor wafted up into my nostrils at the same time I took a deep breath.

It seemed as if the top of my head was coming off, and I was flying higher and higher, Charlene's body wonderfully warm and soft and secure.

Higher and higher I soared, the pleasure coursing through me in gigantic waves, while all the while I was dimly aware that my breath was coming far too fast, and my heart was racing out of control, ready to burst from my chest. And yet the feeling seemed to go on and on, the pleasure rising higher and higher, becoming stronger and stronger, until it was almost pain, but lovely pain, and then stars, and spots, and bright flashes, but all underwater, as if I was drowning . . .

It was daytime. The sun streamed through the
tall windows across the room from my bed, but
there was a deep, rhythmic pounding deep inside
my head. Over and over again, the heavy drumming seemed to throb.

I opened my eyes at length. Slowly and painfully
I sat up in the bed swinging my legs over the edge.

I was alone in the room. Vaguely I remembered
that Charlene had been here last night, but then it
all became a huge jumble.

The drumming continued as I managed to get to
my feet. I stood there swaying for several seconds.
And gradually I began to realize that the drumming sound wasn't inside my head; it was coming
from outside. But far away.

I staggered across the room to where a white
robe was lying over the massage table. I pulled it
on and then went down the corridor and outside on
the porch.

Out here the drums were much louder, and they
seemed to be coming from all directions outside the
town. Out in the jungle. The Indians.

Although I didn't know the exact time, I knew it
was early morning. The sun was just up over the
trees, and the mall was empty of people.

I stepped down off the porch and made my way
down past the fountains in front of the dispensary,
then to Pat's dormitory.

The door was open, and just inside was a counter
behind which were shelves containing sheets and
pillowcases. No one was there.

A set of stairs went up to the second floor, and
beyond the counter was a corridor which ran the

length of the building, doors opening from it at regular intervals. Pat was here someplace, but I didn't have much time to find her. Before long the town would be waking up and I would be missed.

The first door opened to a small room containing four bunks, someone sleeping in each of them.

I crossed the room and bent over the lower bunk to the right and gently shook the woman awake. She blinked her eyes and looked up at me in confusion.

"Is it time for prayers?" she asked.

"Almost," I said softly. "Which room is Sister Pat Staley's?"

"Sister Staley? She's upstairs in twenty-two."

"Go back to sleep," I said. "You'll be awakened when it is time for morning prayers. Peace to you."

"And to you, Brother," the woman said, and she rolled over as I went back out into the corridor and hurried up the stairs.

Pat's room was just across from the stairs and was exactly the same as the other one. I recognized her long blond hair immediately and went to the top bunk where she was sleeping.

She came awake slowly, and when she had finally opened her eyes, she smiled. "Nicky?" she said sleepily.

"It's me, Pat," I said. "Time to go now."

"Go?" she said. "Is it time for prayers?"

"Yes. They sent me to get you. They want us up at the church right away."

"Right now, Nick? I'm so tired."

"Right now," I said. I threw back the covers and lifted her off the bunk. She was nude, her robe lying over the end of the bed.

I helped her pull it on, and then strapped her

sandals on. She was starting to come more awake.

"Are you sure we're supposed to be up at the church so early?"

"Absolutely sure," I said, leading her to the door.

One of the other women woke up and she turned to look at us. "Sister Pat?" she asked sleepily.

"Go back to sleep," I said. "You'll be awakened when it is time for prayers."

The woman sat up. "I know you," she said, loudly. "I know you!"

We had just run out of time. I yanked open the door and hauled Pat out into the corridor and down the stairs.

"Nick, you're hurting me," Pat cried. "What's happening?"

Her roommate came down the stairs behind us. She started screaming, and as we stepped outside we saw someone running down the mall from the Palace of Pleasure.

I picked Pat up, threw her over my shoulder, and raced down toward the docks as her roommate came outside shouting.

"Stop them! Stop them!"

My legs were still weak from the drug, and it was hard to keep my footing. Several other people were shouting at us to stop, and Pat was screaming and crying, pounding at my back with her fists.

At the bottom of the mall, I turned to head across the dock toward the speedboat, but I lost my footing and fell down, my face smashing into the concrete. Pat immediately scrambled away from me.

I jumped up as one of Seidelman's men raced across the dock directly at me. I had just enough time to sidestep his charge and drive my fist into his solar plexus.

He doubled over, and as he started to go down, I hammered both fists into the back of his neck.

Six of Seidelman's goons were on me then, their fists smashing at my face, neck and chest.

Before I went down I managed to kick one of them in the groin, but then a fist the size of a side of beef seemed to materialize out of nowhere. It hammered me in the face and everything went dark. I heard Pat scream somewhere off to my right.

Pat's high-pitched scream seemed to go on and on, echoing inside of my head. Sometimes the sound rose and fell like a siren, and other times I could barely hear it.

I was lying on my back as I finally started to come around. My wrists and ankles were tied down, and my entire body felt like it had been hit by a battering ram.

"He's coming around," a familiar voice said from overhead, and I opened my eyes.

Seidelman and several of his men were standing around me. Seidelman bent closer.

"I'm going to ask you a couple of questions, Carter, and I'm going to want the answers without hesitation or I will kill you here and now." He turned around and rolled a cart closer to the table on which I was lying. We were back in the Palace of Pleasure, only this time there wasn't going to be any pleasure.

Seidelman held up two paddles, each connected to a machine on the cart by thick, coiled wires.

"Do you know what this is?" he asked. "It's a

defibrillation unit used in hospitals the world over to help heart attack victims. The interesting thing about this unit is that it not only starts hearts, it can also stop them. Do you understand what I'm saying?" He reached out and placed the paddles on my chest, and I flinched.

"No juice yet," he said grimly. "The first question. What is your real name?"

I could feel the sweat pouring off me. These were not sane, rational people I was dealing with. "Nick Carter," I said.

"I think I believe that one," Seidelman said. "Who do you work for?"

"Amalgamated Press . . ." I started to say, when Seidelman suddenly nodded his head.

A tremendous jolt bit deeply into my chest. Every muscle in my body contracted, and a massive pain shot through my entire being. Suddenly I could not breathe. A red haze seemed to fill my eyes, and I could feel myself straining against the leather straps holding me in place. I was drowning and unable to come up for air. Someone was saying something to me, but the pain went on and on, and I began to slip away.

A second jolt hammered into my body, my muscles violently convulsing a second time, air rushing into my lungs; and then I was shaking. There was a metallic taste in my mouth, and something was running down the side of my chin.

"He's bitten his tongue," Seidelman said. "Perhaps now he will talk."

Something with an extremely sharp, unpleasant odor was held under my nose, causing my head to clear instantly.

My heart was racing, and my breath was coming in short ragged gasps.

"You were dead there for a few seconds, Carter. I don't expect it was a pleasant experience. Not one you would care to repeat."

The room came back into focus as I was finally able to catch my breath.

"Is the unit recharged and ready?" Seidelman asked.

"Yes, sir," one of the others said.

Seidelman turned back to me and placed the paddles on my chest once again. My muscles jerked involuntarily, and I could feel my bowels loosening.

"Who do you work for, Carter?"

"Security," I mumbled.

Seidelman leaned a little closer. "What was that?"

"National Security Service," I said. It was hard to speak. But I knew my only chance for survival was to tell him something he would believe.

"Is that the Central Intelligence Agency?"

I shook my head. "No . . . no, it's the Justice Department. I work for the Attorney General."

"Now we're getting somewhere," Seidelman said. "Why did you come after the church?"

"Pat was an old friend," I stammered. "She was worried about her brother."

"You weren't sent on assignment?"

"Not at first," I said. "Not until your people tried to kill me. Then I was told I could pursue it."

"Who knows you came here?" Seidelman asked, the first hint of worry on his features.

"My control officer," I said. "No one else."

"The Justice Department doesn't know?"

"No . . . no. I came down here to get Pat. We were going to use her as evidence to close your Chicago operation. We can't do anything to you down here."

"Did Captain Arimá work for you?"

"I hired him in Manaus to take me up here."

"How did you know where we were located?"

"I didn't know, exactly," I said. "We just knew that the church had bought a tract of land down here someplace. I came to find out where. And what was going on."

Seidelman seemed to think for a long moment, and then he pulled the paddles away from my chest, laid them on the machine, and shoved it aside.

"Well, Brother Carter, you're here, and you're definitely going to find out what's going on. You've caused us so much trouble, that we're going to have to close down our operation here and leave." He shook his head. "What most angered us was the way in which you destroyed our equipment over at the dispensary. It is causing us no end of trouble. Trouble for which you will pay dearly." He shook his head again. "In fact, your meddling here will be the cause of nearly everyone's death. It will be on your conscience when you rot in hell."

I closed my eyes, my breathing finally coming more naturally, my heart slowing down.

"Get him ready and then bring him up to the stadium," Seidelman was saying.

"We've never had a daytime ceremony before," one of the other men said.

"It's nearly noon and the tranquilizer is already starting to wear thin on most of our people. We either do it now, or we'll lose the entire shooting match."

"Yes, sir," the other said.

There was silence for a moment, but then Seidelman said, "I want him to participate in the ceremony. But if he tries anything at all, kill him."

"Of course," another man said, and then I could hear someone leaving.

I lay there for several minutes until someone came to my side and undid the straps at my wrists and ankles. I opened my eyes.

There were four men with me, all of them armed. When they had my straps undone, they helped me up off the table and pulled the robe on over my head and strapped sandals on my feet.

My legs were weak, but I pretended not to be able to move at all, and they half carried and half dragged me across the room, down the corridor and outside to the mall.

There were a lot of people outside, many of them milling around the dispensary. Most of them looked confused, as if they didn't know where they were or what they were supposed to be doing.

Several of Seidelman's men were directing people up the wide walkway past the church toward the sports stadium, and as I watched, people began streaming that way.

I could still hear the drums out in the jungle around us, and the high-pitched keening sound was coming from huge loudspeakers high up on the walls of the church.

My guards dragged me off the porch, and we headed up the mall toward the path to the stadium, falling in line with hundreds of others.

I kept searching the faces of everyone around us for a sign of Pat and the boy, Domingo, but they were nowhere in sight.

The stadium was more like an open air church. Tiers of bleachers all faced a steel and glass podium, behind which, at the end of a wide, paved path, was a huge stone altar. Ringing the stadium were powerful lights on tall poles, and around the altar were several pieces of electronic equipment. Evidently the sources of the laser beams we had seen in the sky last night.

The bleachers were already nearly half full when I was dragged to a seat next to the podium. Pat was seated on the other side.

"Nick!" she shouted.

The tranquilizer she had been given was already beginning to wear off. She seemed terrified.

I just smiled at her, and she shook her head in despair.

A ripple of applause began, and it grew into a standing ovation.

I looked over toward the path in time to see Knox, Seidelman, Karsten, and a dozen of their guards, coming from the church.

One of my guards leaned over toward me. "Very soon now, Carter, you're going to get what you came looking for," he said, and he laughed.

As Knox and his retinue came closer, the high-pitched noise from the speakers on the church boomed three times and then suddenly fell silent.

A moment later the drums out in the jungle also fell silent, and the applause stopped.

Out beyond the altar, about two hundred yards away where the clearing met the dense jungle, Indians began stepping out into plain view. There were hundreds of them. They stood there watching us. Waiting.

FIFTEEN

Knox, ringed by his guards, all of them armed with M16s, mounted the dais and faced the bleachers as the last of the people arrived and sat down.

A deep silence had descended over the stadium, in part because of Knox's commanding presence, but also due to the presence of the Indians. There had to be several hundred of them out there now.

"We have come, my brothers and sisters, at long last to the day of the Final Reward," Knox began, his amplified voice booming over the crowd.

The laser beams around the altar flickered on, shooting high up into the clear blue sky.

"The thing we have all striven for, all these years, is joyously at hand. Come! Join me!"

People began getting up and working their way down from the bleachers to stand in a line next to the podium. As each one of them joined the growing group, Knox bent over and said something to them, then kissed them on the forehead.

Music began from hidden speakers, and the laser beams began flashing faster and faster.

When about fifty people had lined up, they

began walking slowly out on the wide path toward the altar.

I started to jump up, but my guard placed the barrel of a pistol against my temple.

"Don't be so anxious to die, Carter," he said softly. "Your turn will come soon enough."

I sank back down.

The first group had reached the altar, and they began climbing up. The first one, an old man, reached the top, turned toward the church, spread his hands, and screamed something.

At that moment, a pencil-thin beam of light, coming from somewhere beneath the altar, pierced the man's chest with a flash, and he crumpled.

The top of the altar was canted backwards, and his body slid, then rolled off to the back.

Two of the natives from the edge of the field raced up to the altar, snatched the body, and then raced with it back to the jungle.

Meanwhile the second person, this one an old woman, had stepped up onto the altar, spread her hands, and died instantly as the laser beam pierced her heart.

Other people were coming down now from the bleachers to stand in line for Knox's blessing. Then they would walk out to the altar where they would die.

The natives, much bolder now, had come closer, and as the second body dropped down to the ground they swooped in, scooped it up, and took it away.

I turned and looked up toward the bleachers. Seemingly everyone was getting to their feet and patiently waiting their turn to come down to the altar to be killed.

It was madness. Insanity.

My guard was prodding my ribs with his pistol. "Now," he said.

I looked at him as four other guards, armed with automatics, came up and motioned for me to get to my feet.

"It's your turn now, Carter," one of them said.

I got to my feet. "Only if I can take Sister Staley with me."

Knox had paused a moment to look down at me. He smiled beatifically and nodded his head. "Of course," he said.

I walked over to the podium where two other guards helped Pat stand, and they brought her over to me. I kissed her on the cheek. "Do exactly as I say," I whispered urgently.

Pat looked up at me, and then Knox was bending down over us.

"Stand on the five-pointed star. Face the church and it will be easy, Brother and Sister. I love you," he said.

He bent farther over and kissed us both on the forehead.

"Peace be with you, Brother Knox," I said.

"And with you," he replied.

Hand in hand, Pat and I turned, stepped outside the line, and started down the path toward the altar.

"Stop them!" someone shouted from behind us.

"Let them go, if they will," Knox's voice boomed.

Everyone stepped aside for us as we approached the altar.

"What are we doing, Nick?" Pat asked, her voice slightly slurred.

"Just do what I say, Pat, and we'll save everyone here," I whispered as we hurried the last few yards along the path.

A young woman had just started up the steps, a deeply terrified expression on her face.

"Let us go first, Sister," I called up to her.

She turned, looked down at us, and then came back down the stairs. She was so frightened, she was hardly able to walk.

Pat and I stepped around her, mounted the steps, and at the top we headed for the star that was etched into the stone.

"We can't do this . . ." Pat started to say, but I shoved her aside, away from the star, as a laser beam flashed from below. I pulled her with me down the steeply sloping side.

A roar went up from the crowd behind us, and Knox's voice was booming over the stadium as we fell to the soft ground below.

I scrambled up to my feet as two Indians, armed with machetes, charged. Sidestepping one of them, I smashed a right hook into the other's face, and he went down in a heap. Spinning around, I was just in time to avoid the first Indian, grabbing his arm as he swung the blade, and breaking it with a sickening snap.

The other Indians, about fifty yards away, stood motionless watching what was happening.

I scooped up one of the machetes and used it to pry off a padlock on a small service door at the base of the altar.

When I had it open, I leaped inside. The altar was hollow and filled with electronic equipment, a large, laser excitation tube pointing upwards at an angle to a hole in the altar floor at the center of the star.

Swinging the machete blade as hard as I could, I cut through the main power cable to the unit, sparks flying everywhere.

"Nick!" Pat screamed.

I spun around and leaped out from under the altar as half a dozen Indians were charging across the field toward us. Pat stood with her back to the altar, a machete in her right hand.

One of Seidelman's guards came around the corner in a dead run, raising his M16 the moment he saw me.

I swung around, flipping the machete at him with every ounce of my strength, the blade nearly burying itself to the hilt in the man's chest.

The instant after he hit the ground, I grabbed his rifle and turned on the Indians, spraying them with two quick bursts.

Several of them went down, and the others turned tail with whoops and shrieks and raced back to the protection of the jungle.

"Get down," I shouted to Pat as I hurried to the corner of the altar.

I looked around just as a group of Seidelman's men, Seidelman in the lead, came charging toward me.

Stepping out away from the altar, I brought the M16 up, and on full automatic, cut all of them down.

Everyone back in the stadium was screaming now, and even Knox's amplified voice was lost in the din.

I raced to where Seidelman and the others had

fallen and grabbed two of their M16s. The people on the path were staring open-mouthed at me, all of them rooted to their spots.

"Get out of here," I shouted. "Everyone back to the church!"

Behind me, the Indians were starting to move in toward the stadium en masse. Pat came around the corner of the altar and I tossed her one of the rifles.

"Get these people up to the church before it's too late," I shouted.

A burst of automatic weapons fire came from the bleachers, and I spun around, dropping into a crouch.

More people were screaming now, but for a frantic second or two I could not see what was happening.

Then a second and third burst of gunfire came from one side of the bleachers, and I could see at least a dozen people going down.

Knox had jumped down from the dais, and now surrounded by his guards, Kenneth Atterbury with them, he was trying to make his way through the crowd heading toward the church, his men shooting anyone who tried to oppose them.

I jumped up and raced directly across the field toward them. I couldn't fire for fear of hitting the people, and yet they had to be stopped. If they made it to the church before the rest of us did, they could close it up, and we would be stuck outside.

The sound of gunfire from behind me brought me around in time to see Pat shooting at a large group of the Indians attacking the people out on the path.

Several of them went down, but then Pat's weapon ran out of ammunition, and two of them leaped at her, their machetes swinging.

I dropped down on one knee, brought the M16 up to my shoulder, and leading the Indians, picked them off one at a time.

Pat raced across the field toward me as more Indians poured onto the field hacking into the crowd with their machetes. People were screaming and blood was flying everywhere.

At least a dozen more Indians broke away and came after Pat. One by one, conserving my ammunition as best I could, I picked them off. Seven of them fell before the others turned and fled back into the melee.

As soon as Pat reached me, we turned and raced up toward the path where Knox and his guards had gone, but they were nowhere in sight now.

Several of the guards had been trampled in the mass exodus, and I stopped to retrieve the clips from their weapons as Pat and I came up to the path leading to the church.

We stopped there, and I turned back, once again dropping to one knee, while taking careful aim at the Indians.

One by one I fired at them, as the last of the people who had managed to get away, streamed past me up toward the church.

Several hundred other Indians had come out of the jungle, and they were dancing around, whooping and screaming, hacking apart the hundreds of bodies on the stadium field, totally oblivious to my firing.

When the last of the congregation had passed us, Pat and I headed back up the path toward the church.

The Indians were cannibals, for whom death was

a religious rite. How much of it was part of their
own heritage and custom, and how much of it was
due to Knox's electronic mumbo jumbo, there was
no way of telling at this point. But I didn't think it
would take them very long to come after the rest of
us.

We made it to the church just as the last of the
people were piling inside, and I went immediately
down the corridor and into the main hall. People
were milling around aimlessly, some of them
screaming and crying, others cursing and shouting
as the tranquilizer they had been on for so long
finally began to wear off, the enormity of the death
and destruction around them, overwhelming.

"Get up on the dais. Find the public address
system and calm these people down," I said to
Pat.

"Where are you going?" she cried, clutching my
arm.

"I've got to get the outer doors closed before the
Indians decide to come up here."

Pat nodded uncertainly.

"Keep your rifle with you in case some of
Knox's guards are in here," I said, and I turned
and went back down the wide corridor to the main
doors.

I stood just outside the doors and looked down
across the deserted mall. No one was in sight, and
below on the dock I could see the power boat still
sitting there. I could hear the frenzied whoops and
screams of the rampaging Indians coming from the
stadium, but from where I stood I could not see
them.

Stepping back inside I swung the massive doors
closed, flipping the simple bar latches over. I could

hear Pat's voice booming over the loudspeakers in the main hall as I hurried around the wide entryway corridor to the side doors. I locked these and did the same with the rear doors and the doors on the opposite side. Only when this was done did I go back into the hall.

The crowd had calmed down now, many of the people sitting down, others perched on the edge of tables as they all listened to Pat up on the dais.

". . . Carter has come to help us get home," she was saying as I threaded my way through the people up to the dais. "But we're going to have to stick together. We have to help him, but most importantly, we cannot panic."

I jumped up on the dais and Pat handed the microphone over to me. I held my hand over it for a moment.

"I've got the doors locked, but if the Indians decide to come up here and break in, we won't be able to stop them."

"What are we going to do?" she asked.

"Get out of here," I said. I raised the microphone and held it up to my lips. "My name is Nick Carter, and I have been sent down here to help you people get home," my voice boomed over the audience. No one said a thing; the great hall was deadly silent.

"But I'll need your help. Has anyone seen Brother Knox?"

"He came in here," a woman near the back shouted. "I saw him and his assistants."

Everyone looked around.

"He's not here in this hall. Has anyone any idea where he might be?"

There was no answer.

"Is there anyone here familiar with this church, with its construction?"

Still there was no answer.

The Indians weren't going to remain down at the stadium for much longer. We had two choices. Either we were going to have to get away from here somehow, or we were going to have to call for help. Either way we'd need a delay.

I glanced at the clear plastic chair that Knox's holographic image had been projected onto, and an idea suddenly came to mind.

"Is there anyone here who knows electronics?" I asked.

An older man in the front row had been leaning against one of the tables. He straightened up. "I do," he said.

"All right. You and I have some work to do. Meanwhile, I want a couple of people at each of the doors to watch for the Indians. If they start up this way, I want to know immediately."

Several men at the fringes of the crowd broke away and headed down the four corridors to the doors.

"Now," I said, "is there anyone here who is wounded or hurt?"

At least twenty hands went up.

"Have we any nurses or doctors here? If so, I want those people taken care of and ready to be moved by nightfall if we have to leave here."

"I'm a nurse," a woman said. "But there are no supplies here. Someone will have to go to the dispensary for them."

"I'll go," Pat spoke up. She still clutched the M16.

There was no other way. I nodded. "Take a couple of the men with you," I said. "And don't be very long about it."

She nodded and jumped off the dais, then picked several men to accompany her. They all headed out of the main hall.

"The rest of you try to get some rest," I said. I laid the microphone down and jumped off the dais.

"Paul Fresnel." The older man who had claimed he knew electronics introduced himself. "What have you got in mind?"

I pointed up at the plastic chair. "Are you aware what that chair is?"

Fresnel smiled. "If you tell me it's some kind of a projector—probably a holograph unit—and that Knox's image was never real, I'd believe you."

I just looked at him in amazement. "If you knew that, why did you go along with all this? The suicides and everything."

Fresnel looked down at his feet and shrugged his shoulders. "Hell, my kids all grew up on me, my wife died five years ago, and I was all alone." He looked up. "No one gave a damn about me, don't you see. Least not until Knox and his crowd came along. Here I belonged and was loved."

I reached out and patted him on the shoulder. "You have a lot of friends now, Paul," I said. "Let's see if we can't get them out of this mess in one piece."

He nodded.

"I want the chair and the projectors moved out into the front corridor directly in front of the main doors. Can it be done?"

Fresnel whistled. "Don't know off hand," he said. He brushed past me, climbed up on the dais, and then inspected the chair and the area around it.

He looked up toward the overhead projector. "We'd have to rip out some of the building's wiring to make up cables. And we'd need some tools."

"Can it be done?"

He looked down at me and smiled. "I'll get on it immediately. But I'll need some help, and like I say, some tools."

"Pick anyone you want to help you, and I'll see if I can find you the tools," I said. "But this is a top priority project. I want that chair in front of the door and ready to go as soon as you possibly can manage it."

"Will do," Fresnel said.

I hurried away from the dais and up the corridor to the front doors. Four men stood by the half-opened doors looking out.

"They made it okay down to the dispensary?" I asked.

One of them looked around and nodded.

"No sign of the Indians?"

"None up here, but we can hear them over at the stadium."

"Keep a close watch," I said. I turned on my heel and went back through the main hall and into the back hall where I punched the button for Knox's elevator.

It was at the top floor, and it took a minute to get down to me. I brought my gun up as the doors opened. There was no one in the car, but there was blood on the floor.

I got in, and as the car rose, I crouched down, the M16's safety off, my finger on the trigger. The woman said she had seen Knox and his men coming into the church. There was a real possibility they were holed up in the apartment.

The doors opened, and I leaped out and rolled to the left. No one was there.

"Knox!" I shouted.

There was no answer. Slowly, covering myself around each corner, I quickly searched the apartment, but without results.

Back in the living room, the elevator door still open, I looked around. There was blood on the floor of the elevator car, but none here on the fur carpeting. They had gotten on the elevator, but they hadn't gotten off up here.

Not up here. They had gone down! There had to be a basement.

I rode the elevator back down to the ground floor. There was a key slot in a control panel, but no buttons.

I stepped off the elevator, let the doors close, then punched the call button again. When the doors reopened, I stepped back on the elevator, and then immediately got off again as the doors closed.

I could hear the elevator car going up. The three men at the back door were watching me, and I called two of them over.

"Help me pry this door open," I said.

The three of us put our shoulders to it, and slowly the door came open to reveal a dark shaft that went down another twenty feet, a door at the bottom.

"When Pat Staley gets back from the dispensary, tell her where I've gone. Knox and his people are down in the basement," I said.

They nodded and went wide-eyed as I slung the M16 over my shoulder and leaped through the open door, grabbing the greasy elevator cables.

I slipped the first ten feet before I was able to get a good grip, but then I was at the bottom.

The door had a release bar, and I slipped it up and opened the door just a crack.

On the other side was a vast, dimly lit room, the thick support columns holding up the church floor above like a concrete forest.

At the far side of the basement there were several strong lights, and I could see several men loading something aboard a forklift truck.

Bringing my M16 around, I eased the door open a little wider, then slipped into the basement. Keeping low and dodging from one support column to another, I worked my way across to within twenty feet of where they were working.

It was gold. In standard bars. There were at least a dozen full pallets of the precious metal and another half a dozen empty ones.

As I watched, the last bars from one of the pallets were loaded onto the forklift, and then the driver maneuvered the heavily loaded machine around a corner and down a wide tunnel.

Gold. They had amassed a fortune down here and now they were moving it out—which meant they had a way of getting out of here.

I stepped out from around the column. "Good afternoon, gentlemen, going somewhere?"

There were four of them sitting on the gold pallets, and at the sound of my voice they all spun around.

At that moment Knox and Atterbury came around the corner from the tunnel. Both of them carried rifles.

"Don't try it!" I shouted, but they started to bring their rifles up. I fired from the hip, at least three hits slamming into Knox's chest, driving him backwards, and two hitting Atterbury.

The other four men all dove toward their weapons a few feet away as I swung the M16 around. On full automatic, I laid down a deadly line of fire.

Three of them went down, but the fourth had reached his rifle as I leaped forward, using my now empty gun as a club.

His rifle was just coming up as I caught him full force on the side of his head with the butt of my own rifle. His skull cracked open, blood spurting everywhere, and he fell over sideways, his legs jerking spasmodically for a few seconds, and then he was still.

Tossing my rifle aside, I grabbed his and raced around the corner into the tunnel which opened about a hundred yards away.

At the end I stopped and looked outside. About a quarter of a mile away, down a long hill, I could see a small force of Indians hacking at something in the forklift. They had been waiting for it and had caught the driver out in the open.

But I now knew how Knox and his men had planned on getting out of here. And I knew how all of us could leave.

Farther down the hill, another quarter mile from the forklift, a Hercules C130 transport aircraft, its rear cargo doors open, sat on a wide runway.

It was our ticket out of here. If we could get to it.

SIXTEEN

With the Indians out there, getting the people across the half mile to the aircraft would be impossible. We didn't have the weapons to fight them off, which left only one other alternative. The Indians would have to be distracted, but long enough for all of us to leave.

I slung the M16 over my shoulder as I hurried back down the tunnel to where Knox lay. He was dead, his eyes open, his lips curled back in a snarl.

He was a large man, and it took me nearly five minutes to drag his body across the basement to the open elevator door.

I stayed there for a moment and caught my breath and then went back and grabbed the other weapons and brought them to the elevator doors.

Inside the shaft, I shouted up to the guards at the back doors, and a few seconds later one of them appeared at the opening above.

"We heard shooting down there," he said.

"Close the elevator door," I shouted up.

"What?"

"Close the elevator door. I'm going to call the car down here. Hurry!"

Once the Indians discovered that the tunnel door was open, they would be coming up here. I didn't want to be caught here totally exposed.

It took several minutes for them to get the door closed above, and when they did, I hit the elevator button and the car started down.

I quickly searched through Knox's pockets and came up with a ring of keys. One of them was undoubtedly for the elevator, and the others were probably for wherever his holographic projector was located.

There was a whoop across the basement and I spun around as dozens of Indians emerged from the tunnel.

They spotted me and headed across in a dead run.

I grabbed one of the M16s and fired a couple of short bursts. Several of the Indians went down, and the others ducked behind the cement columns.

The elevator car arrived, and keeping one eye on the far side of the basement, I dragged Knox's body aboard, then shoved the weapons inside.

I fired another burst as I stepped into the elevator, but the doors wouldn't close. There were no buttons, only the key slot.

Working as fast as I could, I began trying Knox's keys one by one. On the fifth try I had the correct one.

I twisted it over and the elevator door began to close as several Indians made a desperate run at me. I fired again from the hip, but then the door was closed, and I started up with Knox's body and the weapons.

The rear door guards were waiting for me when

the elevator door opened on the main floor. When they saw Knox lying there dead, they all backed up a step.

"Get him off the elevator and find a fresh robe for me," I snapped, stepping out into the corridor.

They were shaking their heads.

"We're getting out of here as soon as it's dark, but we need his body. Now do it!" I shouted.

"What do you want us to do with . . . him . . . when we're done?" one of them asked.

"Leave him here. I'll send someone for him," I said. I hurried across the hall and down the corridor into the main room.

The plastic chair had already been taken off the dais, and Fresnel was directing some people who were pulling wiring from the table lighting fixtures.

I went over to him. "How long before you'll be ready?" I asked.

He looked up, a grin on his face. "A couple of hours at most," he said. He pointed back at the dais where a small service door was open at the base. "We found the equipment room where he sat in front of the projector pickups. The place was filled with tools and almost everything else we needed."

"All right," I said catching my breath. "Just make sure it's ready and in place by dark. We're getting out of here then."

Fresnel nodded.

"When you get a chance, send a couple of your men into the back corridor. We have Knox's body there."

"Body?" Fresnel asked.

I nodded. "There's no time to explain now, but

I want his body propped up in front of the holograph projector pickup as soon as you're ready."

Fresnel nodded nervously, then went back to his work. As I turned around, I immediately spotted Pat across the room where she was helping the nurse tend to the wounded.

I went over to her and took her aside. "Any trouble getting the stuff?"

"No," she said. "Where did you go?"

I quickly explained to her what had happened and what we were going to try to do. She looked scared.

"Will it work?" she asked when I was finished.

"I don't know. But it's the only way out of here as far as I can see," I said. "As soon as possible I want you to start moving everyone out into the back hallway. We're going to leave by the rear doors."

"There are several hundred people here, Nick," Pat said. "Will we be able to get everyone aboard the plane?"

"We'll have to," I said. The plane was one of the largest transport aircraft built. But whether or not we could stuff the large number of people we had into it and still get off the ground was another question.

All through the remainder of the afternoon, Fresnel and his people continued to work on the holograph projectors. Pat and the nurse and a few other women finished with the wounded, and the guards at the doors continued to get more and more edgy.

There had to be hundreds of Indians out there

now, many of them around the Church, but most of them in the town.

For a couple of hours there had been a lot of activity below in the basement. The rear door guards had listened at the elevator door until it finally became quiet below.

The back corridor gradually filled with people from the main hall. Knox's body had been dressed in a fresh robe and was propped in front of the holographic projector equipment beneath the dais.

Pat and four other women worked their way through the crowd, coming up an hour later with an accurate head count and total body weight.

There were four hundred and twenty-seven men and women, including me and the boy Domingo, who had been wounded, but would live, totalling more than seventy thousand pounds. The Hercules would handle it if the runway was long enough and the plane in good shape—and if we could get them all aboard.

A lot of ifs; but I kept telling myself we had no other choice.

It was nearly seven P.M. and dark outside, when at long last Fresnel said we were ready for a test.

"I don't know about the power loss in that long length of makeshift cable," he said. "If it doesn't work the first time, it'll never work."

I found Pat and told her we were ready.

"I'm staying here with Fresnel and two other men until the last one of your people is out the back door and on his or her way down to the airplane. Don't stop for anything, no matter what happens. Get them on board immediately."

"Who's going to fly it?" she asked.

"I am," I said. There was no one else. And although I had never taken off or landed such a big aircraft, I had flown a DC3 once, a number of years ago.

She kissed me on the lips. "I love you, Nicholas," she said softly.

"We're going to take a vacation together when this is over," I said. "Now get everyone ready. We leave in ten minutes."

The guards at the side doors had been pulled away, and I went to the front door where the plastic chair had been set up. Overhead, strung on the ceiling, was the upper projector. The lower unit was on the floor beneath the chair, and the horizontal plane projector was propped on a table to the left. Cables snaked everywhere.

"What's going on outside," I asked one of the guards at the door.

"They're burning the town," he said. "There's hundreds of them out there."

"Let's give them something to celebrate then," I said. "As soon as Knox's projection comes to life, I want you to open the doors, then get back with the others. As soon as it's clear at the rear of the building, get everyone down to the airplane."

They all looked at me nervously for several seconds, but then they nodded.

Fresnel and I went back to the equipment room beneath the dais. Knox's body was seated stiffly in the chair, his eyes still open, his lips still curled back into a death mask grin.

"He offered us hope for a better world," Fresnel said looking at him. "The Final Reward, it was called. A final reward for a life of toil."

"He was a madman," I said softly.

Fresnel looked up at me. "We all were, Mr. Carter, we all were." He flipped several switches, and the equipment came to life, casting an eerie blue-tinged light on the corpse.

"It's now or never," Fresnel said. He hit the main power switch, the blue glow intensifying to a bright, hard blue light.

Someone came running from the front hall. "He's there . . . I mean it's working."

"Right," I said. "Get back with the others now, Paul. I'll come along as soon as the last one is out."

Fresnel clapped me on the shoulder, then left. I picked up the microphone and stepped to the service door. From there I could hear the natives screaming from the open front doors.

The remainder of the guards burst from the corridor, raced across the main hall, and were gone, leaving me alone.

"Greetings my children, this is the voice of God!" I said in Portuguese. I could hear my voice booming throughout the church, and when I stopped I could no longer hear the natives outside. They were all quiet. They understood.

"Gather, my children, gather at my feet and I will tell you the word of all the gods. Gather, my children, and hear my words."

I held the microphone in one hand, the M16 in the other, Knox's corpse behind me as I spoke. I had no way of knowing what was going on outside, and I would have to remain here until someone came back for me with the news that everyone had gotten out of the building. In the meantime, I was going to have to hold the Indians in front of the projection of Knox's body.

"Come my children," my voice boomed. "Drop your tools of war, and hear my message."

Except for my own greatly amplified voice, I could hear nothing else. I spoke on and on, exhorting the Indians to gather at the front of the church, to look at Knox's image, to listen to his words.

At one point I invited the bravest of the Indians to come forward and touch my body. And then I stopped talking until from somewhere in the front hallway, I heard a man scream.

One of the Indians had evidently done what I had asked and had come to try and touch the body that wasn't there.

"I am God, and you will listen!" I shouted.

Pat suddenly appeared around the corner of the dais. "They're on their way," she said.

I nodded. "Listen to my words inside of you. Gaze now on my face and learn the word of God," I roared.

I laid the microphone down, jumped out of the equipment room, and both of us hurried across the main hall, down the corridor and out the back door.

The night was hot and very muggy as we ran down the path that led into the jungle.

By the time we made it down to the plane, the last of the people were climbing aboard.

"Make sure everyone is in, and then come forward; I'll need your help," I said.

Pat helped the people climb aboard as I worked my way forward to the cockpit. They were all crammed into the aircraft, shoulder to shoulder, with no room to move let alone sit or lie down.

I climbed into the left-hand seat, studied the instrument panel for several long seconds, and then flipped on the master switch and the panel lights.

The instrument gyros came to life, and the fuel gauges on a back panel where the flight engineer would normally sit, came up to full.

One by one, I kicked the engine preheaters, fuel pumps, and then the starters, each engine slowly grinding to life. Oil and hydraulic pressures all came up to the green marks as I steadied the RPMS to one thousand.

Pat came screaming into the cockpit. "Everyone's aboard, but the Indians are coming down from the church!"

"Strap yourself in," I snapped, and I looked over my shoulder at the engineer's panel, finally finding the cargo bay door control. I hit the switch, and I could hear the dull vibrations of the cargo doors closing. A minute later the indicator light winked green above the CARGO DOOR CLOSE position.

Flipping on the landing lights, I released the parking brake, advanced the throttles and propeller pitch controls, and we began to move.

The plane had been lined up on the end of the runway, and hesitating only a moment to make sure all the gauges were indicating the proper readings, I shoved the throttles and pitch controls all the way forward, and we were rolling. We moved slowly at first as we bumped down the runway, but then we began to gather speed. I added fifteen degrees of flaps three quarters of the way down the runway, the nose coming up slightly.

And then we were rotating, angling back almost

on our tail. The ground suddenly dropped away beneath us, and the dark jungle stretched out for hundreds of miles in every direction, as we ponderously fought for altitude.

Landing was going to be a problem, but one that could be solved with a sharp air controller who could talk me down. It would probably be to the east somewhere, in Peru, a friendly country.

But we had made it. Now it would only be a matter of the Justice Department mopping up the final details of the church's operation in Chicago, and for the people back in the cargo hold to somehow go back to their normal lives.

Others would help with that, though.

As soon as I got home, however, I was going to make good my promise to Pat, and take her on a vacation. A very long vacation.

DON'T MISS THE NEXT NEW
NICK CARTER SPY THRILLER

THE MENDOZA MANUSCRIPT

Once again he began to choke on his blood and his body was wracked by what must have been an unbearable spasm of pain, because he opened his mouth and tried to speak.

I leaned over and said, "Go ahead, Alexi, I'm listening."

"Phone . . ." he whispered. "Phone . . . call . . ."

"You knew I was here from a phone call?" I said, and he nodded almost imperceptibly.

"The way we found out," Jennifer said.

"Who else is in town, Alexi?" I asked.

He closed his eyes, as if just considering the question was causing him great pain.

"G-Germans . . ." he moaned. "Von . . . Von Sydow . . ."

"Eric Von Sydow," I said. That was bad. Von Sydow was even more dangerous than Alexi who, were it not for a loose board, might have killed me just moments ago, and Jennifer.

"W-working . . . to-together . . ." he said, meaning he and the German had been working together, which I knew wouldn't have lasted. If and when they had gotten to the book, one would certainly have killed the other.

"Who else, Alexi?"

"Free-freelancers . . ." he stammered, which made sense. Mendoza was the greatest agent-for-hire of all. Freelancers would be coming out of the woodwork on this one, not only to make money, but to make a name for themselves.

"K-Kolof . . . Pisier . . . Steinbrunner . . ."

Dangerous men, all of them. Ivan—pronounced E-von—Koloff was Polish, but gave his allegiance to the highest bidder, as did the rest. Pisier, the Frenchman, loved women and needed money to buy them with. He also loved killing. I would have bet that he was behind the first attempt on me. When it came to killing, he generally made the first move.

The name that I liked the least was Steinbrunner, Christian Steinbrunner. He did not look like a dangerous man, which made him even more so. Brought up in Switzerland, he did this kind of work mainly because it made him feel alive, and because he made a lot of money at it. Steinbrunner would have to be the second best freelancer behind Mendoza. A year ago I would have placed him third, but a man had died last year, which had moved Steinbrunner up to the number two spot.

So, with Alexi out of the picture, I still had to deal with Von Sydow, Koloff, Pisier and Christian Steinbrunner—and those were only the evils that I knew about. Who knew how many others were floating around. Pretty soon we'd all have to end up in the same spot, and the one left standing would get the book—if that one could get it from

Ric Mendoza. He'd be smart just to sit back and watch us all knock each other off, and then deal with the winner.

"Please," Alexi said suddenly. "Please . . ."

He was in exquisite pain, and he was begging me to keep my part of the bargain.

"Nick, you can't," Jennifer told me, touching my arm.

I looked at her, then back down at Alexi, who was watching me closely. He desperately wanted out of his misery. As I put my gun back in my shoulder holster, his eyes widened in surprise and Jennifer expelled a sigh of relief. When she turned her back to leave, I picked up Alexi's fallen rifle and killed him.

—From THE MENDOZA MANUSCRIPT
A New Nick Carter Spy Thriller
From Ace Charter In September